An entrepreneur, filmmaker, and photographer, **Varun Agarwal** is now an author. When not arguing with Anu Aunty, he is busy running his three companies in Bangalore.

For more details on the author, visit:
http://www.facebook.com/anuauntybook
http://www.facebook.com/varun.agarwal1
http://www.twitter.com/varun067

Praise for

How I Braved Anu Aunty and Co-Founded
a Million Dollar Company

'Vibrant and inspiring.'
—*The Times of India*

'A book that you can connect with.'
—*The Hindu*

'A story about achieving your dreams and living it.'
—*The Deccan Chronicle*

'A true story about going after your dreams.'
—*Outlook India*

'Inspiring the young to reach for the stars. A true success.'
—*The Indian Express*

'Fascinating and entertaining.'
—*The India Today Group*

HOW i BRAVED ANU AUNTY & CO-FOUNDED A MILLION DOLLAR COMPANY (a true story)

Varun Agarwal

RUPA

Published by
Rupa Publications India Pvt. Ltd 2012
7/16, Ansari Road, Daryaganj
New Delhi 110002

Sales centres:
Allahabad Bengaluru Chennai
Hyderabad Jaipur Kathmandu
Kolkata Mumbai

ISBN: 978-81-291-1979-7

Seventh impression 2014

10 9 8 7

The moral right of the author has been asserted.

Printed at Shree Maitrey Printech Pvt. Ltd., Noida

Dear Mum,

If you ever find this book, don't read beyond this point. If you do, please don't disown me. You know I love you.

Sincerely,
Varun

Disclaimer

All the opinions expressed in this book are my own and are a result of the way in which my highly filmy mind interprets a particular situation. If I have inadvertently and unintentionally hurt someone through this book, well, too bad! Like always, I blame the heavy dose of Bollywood I grew up on for the over-the-top drama found in my writing.

Contents

Part 2

Part 3

'Dude, This Guy Can't Write for Shit'

So before I start, I want to tell you that this book narrates the true story of my journey of becoming an entrepreneur. Okay, fine, maybe some aspects of my personal life are a bit exaggerated, but this is my story. So, take it or leave it.

This book simply relates all the experiences that I've been through while trying to start my company with my friend, Rohn Malhotra.

People close to me know I am no writer. However, while writing this book, I really tried my best to stir up the inner Hemingway in me. But that's where the problem lies. You see, there IS no inner Hemingway in me!

So please don't read the book and then go running around like an enthu cutlet*, telling your friends: 'Dude, I read this book; it's a good story but the guy can't write for shit.' I know that.

My former English teacher is probably going to scream after reading this. I am a storyteller and not a writer, so don't expect much.

(The names of some of my friends have been changed at their request.)

---

*Enthu cutlet is a typical Bangalore word and refers to someone who gets over-excited about a variety of things like landing up at a restaurant before anyone else, making party plans on every occasion or even otherwise and putting up a status update on Facebook every two hours.

Part 1

'He Got Only 95 per cent, Ya'

I have a vivid memory of my first encounter with Anu Aunty. I was in the sixth grade and my mum had come to school to collect my report card. Mum had met her at a random kitty party and they struck up a friendship that lasts till date— ruining me in the process. While at school, I was always on the average side when it came to studies, and had no qualms about it. But that was before Anu Aunty breezed, or rather, thundered into my life.

After collecting yet another disappointing report card, my mum was heading towards the door when she bumped into Anu Aunty. She was one of those women who always poked her nose into everyone else's problem and sniffed for one even when there was none. She walked with an air of importance and pretended to know everything. She spoke in this characteristic sing-song style that never failed to annoy me.

'Poo, haw are you ya?' she gave my mum, Poornima, a friendly thwack with her heavyset arm. My mother quickly hid my report card in the folds of her sari and beamed.

'I'm good, Anu,' she said. 'I didn't know your son studies here. What a pleasant surprise.'

Hmm…I didn't quite buy this. You see, Indian aunties always know what other aunties are up to, what their children do, how much their husbands earn, the latest dish they have learnt to cook, and a billion other things that will make your head spin.

'I know ya. It is a pleasant surprise. So how did he do?' Anu Aunty was salivating with curiosity.

Okay, this was the bad part. Aunties hate it when they don't have a good comeback.

I had never given my mum a reason to boast about me and this moment couldn't get worse.

'You know how these boys are ya,' my mother put on a tragic face. 'They don't study only.' She looked at me accusingly, as though I had just failed the IIT entrance. I was eleven years old, for God's sake!

'But how has your Arjun done, Anu?' my mum asked.

Arjun was the blue-eyed boy of our class and the apple of teachers' eyes. He could have an orgasm at the mention of exams and read textbooks with the same eagerness one reserved for *Penthouse*. He would always be interested in how much I had scored, pissing me off mightily. You remember that nerd in your school who would raise his hand every time a teacher asked a question? Arjun was that fucking nerd.

'Oh! Arjun hasn't done well this time, ya Poo. I'm really surprised by this boy.' Anu Aunty sighed.

I smiled for the first time that day. What? A glimmer of hope? Maybe for once he screwed up?

'How much did he score, Anu?' my mum asked with renewed enthusiasm.

'Only 95 per cent.' Anu Aunty shook her head in dismay.

That is when I was introduced to the devious and sadistic world of Anu Aunty. She had this innate ability to make you feel extremely bad about yourself. 95 per cent not only implied that Arjun had topped the class, but the entire sixth grade as well.

'Haw, but that's brilliant ya, Anu.' My mother looked so impressed that one would think Arjun had received the Nobel Prize. I wondered fleetingly if this would be a good time to break the news that my Maths teacher wanted to meet my parents next week.

'No ya, Poo, I had set a target of 98 per cent for him. He knows very well he is not getting his G.I. Joe now.'

Who the fuck scores 95 per cent and asks for a G.I. Joe?

Anu Aunty wagged her fat finger at me. 'Varoon, you need to study hard, son. Stop giving your mum so much trouble ya. Remember, no studies, no future. Anyways, chalo, I'll go now. Have to drop Arjun for his violin classes also.'

And with that Anu Aunty turned around and left us in the dust. My mum was awestruck. It was as if Virendar Sehwag had met Sachin Tendulkar for the first time. What was worse, she wanted to turn me into Arjun's clone now.

Noon Wines—Scene 1

It was the summer of 2009 and I had just come back from Mumbai after a small holiday. Rohn Malhotra, aka Mal, a close friend of mine from school, had just finished writing his GMAT exams. Having scored an enviable 740, he deemed it extremely necessary to get wasted one night and called everyone to Noon Wines.

Noon Wines is one of Bangalore's oldest pubs and the chicken pakodas and beer there are to die for. Of late this has become a pre-party hub, attracting a lot of hot girls who in turn attract a lot of desperate guys like us.

Since 'chicks' were always in attendance, I wasn't surprised to find Devika there. Devika was the resident hottie at Sophia High School, and had been on the mind of every puberty-hitting student at Bishop Cotton Boys' School back in the days. In fact, catching a glimpse of Devika before exams was considered auspicious by many. Manjeet, a close Surd friend of mine, even held the unique distinction of shaking her hand once! She was tall, very pretty and had a child-like innocence about her. Her eyes were so mesmerising, they could cast a magical spell on those that met their gaze.

So anyway, to take our story forward, I was the first one to reach Noon Wines and was, as usual, kept waiting. What was worse was that I had been played in by the 'Dude, be there in two minutes' rule. Well, the rule is if your friend claims he is on the way, and is X minutes away, you simply add fifteen to it. Thus, I did something that I knew would make everyone hurry up.

'Dude, where you?' I asked one of my friends.

'On my way bro, will be there in five minutes,' he said.

'Dude, come fast. Devika is here.'

'Whaaat? I'm coming now, Bob,' he shrieked and hung up.

It is very interesting to note the use of the word 'Bob' here. This varies in different parts of the country. Down south we have 'macha', up north we have 'bhai', 'man' is applicable all over India—but 'Bob' is something you'll hear only in Bangalore. Something like, 'Hey Bob, check out the low-cut that Neha is wearing, Bob.'

So, the boys finally rounded up, pitchers were ordered, cigarettes were lit and the conversation started flowing. There was Rohit to my left, currently working at Oracle, and extremely pissed with his life. He had secured a top rank in his CET and had aced his engineering, but had since receded out of the limelight. His only shot at redemption was to get a 770 in GMAT, which he was still trying hard to achieve. He looked like a cross between actor Shakti Kapoor and John Lennon, except for the fact that he was way shorter. He was the obedient kid who wanted to do an MBA, then hopefully land a job in the Silicon Valley, get married to a homely-comely girl and live happily ever after.

To my right was Sid—ex-Loyola, ex-LSE, topper at Cotton and now without a job. Sid was a victim of recession and would usually be found at Satya's Bar and Restaurant drowning his sorrows in copious amounts of Blender's Pride. His parents were in Chennai and the PG (Paying Guest house) he lived in had witnessed many a scandalous thing—stuff I can't talk about in this book.

Sid looked like a South Indian Paul McCartney, and had trapped quite a few unsuspecting South Indian girls with his boyish charm. Always the one to get into trouble, or get someone else into trouble, Sid was still that one guy you could count on at any time.

Then there was good old Gujju Boy, Mehta. A mechanical engineer by choice, Mehta was trying his best to avoid an early Gujju wedding by doing what every Indian does best— pursue his studies in the US of A. He was more likely to get a hard-on reading an MIT brochure than a *Playboy*. Mehtu would definitely be the George Harrison of Gujarat. And surprisingly, knew more Kannada than the rest of us!

And finally, there was Mal. He was a typical coolio, the kind of guy who'd photocopy notes to study before his final exams. He was working in KGMP and his future was all chalked out to earn an MBA abroad. Extremely enterprising, Mal was that guy who could make you treat him on his own birthday.

One great thing about Bangalore is its thriving pub culture and the endless flow of delicious golden draught beer, and our waiter, Nagesh, kept them coming. As we consumed pitcher after pitcher, the conversation was bound to heat up.

'Dude Mal, how the fuck did you manage a 740, you slut?' Rohit quipped, clearly smarting from his own failure in the GMAT.

'Eh, chill scenes dude. Just write it with a clear head.'

You see, that's Mal. He'll make everything seem like a walk in the park.

'What shit, man. I know how much you fuckin' studied for this shit,' said Sid, venting his own frustration at not finding a job.

'Guys, what is wrong with you all? Mehta banged his fist on the table. 'Why the fuck is everyone talking about studies?' He snapped his fingers at the waiter. 'Aye, Nags. *Illi beer kodu pa.*' Mehta's Kannada was becoming even better than his Gujarati. But what was astonishing was that, for once, he didn't want to talk about studies.

In the midst of all this, Mal and I stepped out to Raju's for a quick smoke. There was this idea that had been brewing in my head for a long time and I really wanted to talk to Mal about it. Almost a year back, my cousin from Mumbai had showed up at our house for a vacation. He was an ex-Mayo grad—Mayo College is one of the oldest and most prestigious boarding schools in India—and would always flaunt his school's sweatshirt, indirectly mocking me for having studied in a 'lesser' school.

The number of school souvenirs he had with the word 'Mayo' on them blew a bulb in my head. What if I could make a business out of this?

Mal and I had met in the eleventh grade in school. We had done numerous school plays together and were the reigning quiz champs of our batch. When I started making short films in college, we usually fine-tuned the concept and the script together, and more often than not, he ended up acting in my films. Besides, like I said, he was one of the most enterprising guys I knew. So it seemed logical for me to talk to him about this 'idea' that had been in my head for a long time now. Raju's boys handed us our ciggies and with a mug of beer in one hand and a Mild in the other, I asked Mal, 'So Mal, what's your scene now, da?'

'Nothing dude,' he said. 'I'll mostly apply for MBA this year. Next year, I'm out of the country, bro.'

'So we have a year?'

'A year? For what?'

Looking back, I can't believe it started like this.

'Mal, I have an idea I want to run by you,' I said.

'Sure bro, tell me.'

'Dude, but we have to give this a shot, no matter what.'

'You know we always do, you fuck.'

'OK. Two words—School Merchandising.'

'Keep talking.'

'OK, so we make hoodies, tees, etc. for the alumni of schools and colleges. And we also make batch hoodies, batch tees, etc. for the passing-out batches of these institutions.'

Until then, there were some small business outfits who were doing this in India, but it had all been random. A brand had never been created for this segment and that's exactly the space I wanted us to fill.

So basically, the idea was to create a brand out of school and college merchandising. Pretty much like those Harvard and Stanford hoodies. Except that we would make these for Indian schools and colleges.

'I like it,' Mal said, giving me a high-five and letting out a wisp of smoke into the night air.

'You think we should do it?' I asked, my heart thudding.

After a pause of almost thirty seconds he finally said, 'Yeah man, let's start working on it right away.'

Typical Mal. Not only did he 'get' the idea, but he also spun it around in his head and did a whole SWOT (Strengths, Weaknesses, Opportunities and Threats) analysis like a hotshot MBA he was aspiring to become.

However, the only downside to all this was—we were extremely wasted.

Thus, under the influence of huge amounts of fresh Kingfisher draught beer, we started doing what every drunk guy with a business idea in a bar does. We took a piece of tissue paper, duly supplied by Nagesh, along with his own 'lucky' pen. As Mal and I scribbled away, the lanky waiter with shifty eyes kept peeping over us, trying to figure out what was going on. Rohit, Sid and Mehta were too wasted at this point to talk about anything except pussy and while they regaled each other with tales of debauchery, Mal and

I worked on a so-called 'business plan'. Charts were made, numbers were jotted down and Nagesh went on to comment, for some strange reason, that we reminded him of Amitabh Bachchan and Shashi Kapoor. In the excitement of putting everything down, I saw ourselves as the next Steve Jobs and Steve Wozniak, though I knew that was a stretch.

Noon Wines—Scene 2

Usually the ritual in Bangalore is to get wasted on a Friday night, avoid the cops and crash at someone's place to roll a joint. Rains are always unpredictable in this city and it was pouring by the time we stepped out. Rohit started complaining that he wanted to go home while Sid and Mehta were getting drenched in the rain, singing some weirdly sexual Bollywood number. My stomach was, meanwhile, giving me trouble and I knew I shouldn't have drunk that last pitcher. As we dumped everyone in one piece into my car, we sped off into the dimly lit streets of Bangalore like 'Roadside Romeos', where the chances of running into a cop were extremely high.

Roadside Romeos are a bunch of jobless guys all huddled together in a car trying to impress random women on the road.

Suddenly, Sid shouted, 'STOP!', and then proceeded to puke all over Mehta. While Mehta started taking blind swings at Sid, Rohit's mother called, her frantic voice clearly audible to all of us. And just when we thought things couldn't get worse, the cops caught us.

Getting caught by cops is a tradition for every self-respecting youngster in Bangalore. Even if you drank as much as a lousy pint, you could find yourself in the ever-widening trap of the cops at night. All of us had broken our cherry long back and even though getting caught was no big deal, however, you could have your car seized if you ran into an inspector.

A six-foot cop with a lush moustache that resembled the Amazon jungle, peered down and knocked on my window.

'Hello Saar. Blow please in the meter,' he instructed me. Another cop, probably his lackey, stood next to him with a notepad and pen.

Now usually the limit is 40 on this stretch. If you show an 80, you could get off by paying five hundred bucks. If you touch 120, there could be some trouble, but they take more money and let you go. But the problem was, I was touching frickin' 180! I had failed the breathalyzer test.

'Oh Saar, very drunk. Come out with laicense please,' said the man with the exhilaration of an FBI official having caught an international criminal.

As I stepped out, I noticed the inspector giving me dirty looks. Mal also got out of the car and tried to reason with the other cop in a slurry tone.

The inspector looked menacingly at me. 'Student, ah?'

I kept quiet and stared at my red Converse sneakers just like I had done during my viva exams.

He stroked his bushy mustache and growled. 'Aye rascal, student ah?'

I just graduated from engineering you fucker, I almost blurted out. Thankfully, I was too drunk to speak.

This time he screamed, 'Aye rascal, wopen youver mouth I say.'

I obeyed and puked all over his white shirt.

You know, there are some moments in your life that you never ever forget. I was just experiencing one such moment. I hate to sound like a Bollywood film, but time actually stood still. Like literally.

So anyways, this sobered everyone down except Sid, who continued to scream 'Kajarare' in the presence of the cops. Mal took the inspector aside and tried to calm him down. But the guy had just been puked upon, so there was no way he was going to let us go and Sid's rendition of 'Kajarare' was certainly not helping. All of us emptied our pockets one by one, and we finally ended up paying five thousand bucks for our shenanigans. Ironically, two years later, we took part in the Anna Hazare rally.

Not much was spoken on our way back. I had pulled out whatever tissue paper I had from my pocket to wipe my face and tossed them out of the window. Yes, including the one with our business plan on it.

'What Varooon, Still Sleeping at this Time?'

I woke up the next morning, rather afternoon, with a really bad hangover. Lalit, my cook cum brother-in-arms cum agony aunt, was waiting at the foot of my bed with a cup of tea in his hands. A native of Bihar, Lalit has been our cook for a long time. He is a big fan of Sunny Deol and still harbours dreams of becoming an actor one day.

I took a sip of tea and made my way to the hall. I froze in my tracks when I saw a familiar portly figure in my drawing room. It was Anu Aunty engaged in serious gossip with my mum! And it wasn't hard to guess they were discussing me.

'I'm very worried ya Anu. This boy is not taking any responsibility only. He sleeps at three, wakes up at one,' my mum said.

'Poo what are you saying? Haww.' Anu Aunty's chignon wobbled as she shook her head.

'I don't know what to do only ya,' my mother sniffled. 'Can you please help me get this boy on track?'

Oh shit. I was doomed.

'Don't worry, Poo. Now that you've asked me, I'll make sure our Varun is back on track.' Anu Aunty sounded determined. Her large red bindi and fiery orange sari set the room ablaze. I broke out in a cold sweat.

These were dangerous shores and I knew I had to get back to the safety of my room. But just as I was going to escape, they caught me, as though I was a CIA agent who had just chanced upon a conversation amongst the mujahideen or something.

'What Varooon, still sleeping at this time ya?' quipped Anu Aunty with a newfound authority over me.

Still sleeping? Had she and my mum only known what had happened last night...

'Uh aunty, no, was uh…' I fumbled.

'Ya, ya. I know everything. Your mother is telling me about you. Sleeping at three, waking up at one. Till when will this go on ya? And what's that shabby hair on your chin?' she demanded, referring to my goatee.

'Uh…no aunty. I woke up at eleven yesterday.' I smiled sheepishly and ran my fingers through my hair.

'You should see Arjun,' said Anu Aunty. 'He is up sharp at six, goes for a jog and then work.'

Yeah, right, the guy has never had a girlfriend in his life, doesn't drink, doesn't go out, doesn't live! He asked for a G.I. Joe when he got a 95 per cent, so he is bound to wake up at six.

'And what are you planning to do with your life now Varoon?' Anu Aunty's shrill voice drilled through my head. 'Why don't you speak to Biju Uncle?'

I winced. Biju Uncle is Anu Aunty's husband. The guy convinced my mum to push me into science for grades eleven and twelve, which I fucking hated. He then convinced my mum to push me into engineering, which I fucking hated even more. God knows what he must be scheming now.

While Anu Aunty and my mum were conspiring to get me back on 'track', I cooked up some excuse and made a dash for the door. This lady was an omnipresent force in my life, sometimes more so than my mother, and derived some sadistic pleasure from meddling in my affairs. I think she enjoyed the fact that her son was doing better than me.

While I did run away from her; life was closing in on me. I had finished my engineering almost a year back and was pretty much jobless since then. I had been an average student at best, and most of all, couldn't bear the thought of joining a tech company. My parents were not particularly happy with me, especially since all my friends were either working or pursuing 'higher studies'. I was the black sheep, the bad apple, and to make matters worse; I was a Maroo (Marwari). This worried my mum even more because that put me out of the reckoning for a hefty dowry. However, for as long as I can remember, I had always wanted to start something of my own.

The entrepreneurial bug had bitten me first when I was merely eight years old. My mum had once baked brownies for me and packed some in my school tiffin box. They were really tasty and I was having a go at them during recess, when Karan Dutta, a good friend of mine and someone known for his gastronomical pursuits, sauntered to my desk.

'Aye, give no, little,' he said, his tongue sticking out.

'Mad uh, I just have one piece left,' I mumbled between bites, hiding my only remaining brownie from his view.

'Aye please da, small piece da.'

'Sorry,' I said, too greedy to care.

'I'll give you two rupees,' Arjun pleaded.

I stopped mid-bite and instinctively knew the moment had to be milked. I allowed my Maroo instincts to take charge. I sold the last one to Arjun and brought a whole box of brownies the next day. After making money from my entire class, I had dreams of selling brownies to the entire school. But that plan was stalled as soon as my mum got wind of my 'business'. However, I was pleased with the twenty-five rupees I had already made—a princely sum for a kid in the fourth grade.

But in this country, it's a crime if you want to do anything apart from becoming an engineer or a doctor. The word entrepreneur practically doesn't exist, and if you want to do something on your own, you're treated like a terrorist.

After the run-in with Anu Aunty, I kept staring at the ceiling fan. Like for hours. I was becoming an expert at that sort of thing. I'd lie for hours looking at the ceiling fan and just think. Myriad thoughts would race through my mind about how dysfunctional this society of ours had become by not allowing one to do what one really loved.

But when you're that jobless, there's another thing that you end up spending most of your time on—FACEBOOK.

This social networking phenomenon has single-handedly caused the collective output of our entire generation to be reduced by half. Whether he is at work, at home, or plain right jobless like I was, there's one thing every guy uses to 'stalk' girls—Facebook. Now the funny thing is, no matter how much you hate to admit it, you always end up 'stalking' your friends' pretty female friends. You end up seeing their photos, their likes, their info, and then you stumble upon their other pretty female friends and it goes on and on. The smartest thing Facebook has done is to never reveal who visited your profile. I would have never been able to see Devika's profile otherwise. I checked her profile constantly. My heart melted every time I saw her beautiful black-and-white profile photo. I also couldn't take my eyes off her diamond nose ring and the small tattoo on her lower back.

Yeah, I know. I saw all three hundred and sixty-seven pictures of hers, so? Like you haven't 'Facebook stalked' someone before?

Call me old-fashioned, but there's something about a nose ring and a tattoo on a South Indian Brahmin girl that simply makes her irresistible, divine almost. I had been thinking of adding her as a 'friend' for some time now, but didn't have the balls to do it. Besides, despite having a lot of mutual friends, she could have considered me creepy. After all, I was a jobless loser with nothing much to speak of.

While I was busy admiring Devika's tattoo, Mal pinged me:

'Dude, you alive?' he wrote.

'Ha ha, just about, Mal.'

'Let's meet for chai and smoke?'

'Cool. When bro?'

'I finish work at seven. Meet me at Shiva's?'

Shiva's is a tea joint in our neighborhood. Nothing ever beats the heady combination of some spicy hot Shiva's tea, a Classic Mild and obviously, Bangalore's beautiful weather. The owner, Shiva, and his waiters were an enterprising lot, men after my own heart. When the song 'Sutta na Mila' (yeah, the one with all BCs and MCs in it) was at its peak, they used to play it in a loop, inducing their customers to smoke longer, thus increasing their sales.

Mal showed up on time and we sat down with our chai and smoke.

'Bad scene last night, dude.' I said.

'I know man,' said Mal. 'My mom caught me when I went home. Faak.' Mal getting caught was very rare.

'I got belted today afternoon man,' I took a drag of my cigarette. 'And bloody Anu Aunty was at home.'

Mal laughed, almost choking on his tea. 'Anu Aunty? Dude, you must have got so fucked, eh?' All my friends knew her; she had attained some sort of folklore status.

'Fuck it dude. Do you remember our talk last night?'

'I don't get high on a couple of beers like you do,' Mal grinned.

'So, what do you think?' I asked.

'I think we should do it,' he said, sealing our destiny that was just beginning to take shape.

This was the grand idea: We would start a company that would make merchandise for the alumni of schools and colleges, and also provide this to the student community at large. Yes, we had a great idea. But that's also where everything usually stops.

The difficult reality is that every great idea needs money. We imagined we would open retail stores across the country, stocking them with the merchandise of schools and colleges of that city. But such a project would involve massive investment. Mal worked at KGMP and I was a jobless fuck. No one in their right mind would invest in us. There was also no question of hitting our families or friends for a loan. So we had to figure out innovative ways to do this on our own, where we wouldn't have to rely on anyone except ourselves.

Mal and I planned to meet up soon and take this further. All of us have had moments where we drink and come up with some crazy business ideas. Numbers are projected, business plans are made, but the next day the idea usually fizzles out with the hangover. I could only hope that this didn't turn out to be one of those ideas.

'Chickoo, Play Violin, na. Show Uncle and Aunty'

A few days passed in a limbo. Mal got caught up with a project at work and our 'idea' was temporarily stalled. I feared that our idea would die a natural death soon, and just when things were getting worse, mum suddenly barged into my room.

'Varun, we're going to Anu's house for dinner beta,' she announced.

'Whaaaat? Ma, there's no way I'm coming. No. Way.'

'You *have* to come, Varun. Aunty has invited you so many times. It's Arjun's birthday. Even Biju Uncle wants to meet you.'

Holy shit! Even Biju Uncle wants to meet me? If I can't wriggle out of this one, I am royally screwed.

'Ma, I can't come,' I said in my firmest tone. 'I have lots of work.'

Facebook is work too, right?

'OK fine. Don't come,' my mother said in a defeated voice. 'I'll go alone. It is so far and it will get so late. But I will drive alone. Don't worry Varun, you do your work.'

You see, that's where Bollywood has spoilt this country. Indian mothers have learnt the art of emotional blackmail from all those movies from the '70s, which they use at will on their kids. There is absolutely no weapon against this and one has no option but to listen to what they say.

I sulked through the drive to Anu Aunty's house. Tortured moments of a shared childhood with Arjun zipped through my mind. Do you remember those times when as a kid, if you had any special talent, your parents would parade you in front of guests and make you display your talent and get some sick pleasure out of it? Thankfully, I had no such talent, a fact which caused my mum to hang her head in shame on many an occasion. Once when I had tagged along with my parents to Anu Aunty's place for a party, Biju Uncle had egged on his son to play whatever little he knew on the violin.

'Chickoo, play on the violin, na. Show uncle and aunty,' he said.

'No Papa, not now,' Arjun replied.

'Chickooo, chalo now!' Biju Uncle growled in his 'play-now-or-you-will-die' tone. So obviously, poor Chickoo had no option but to play. And as expected, he didn't soothe our ears with Chopin or Mozart, but played the signature tune from *Dilwale Dulhaniya Le Jayenge*, much to everyone's excitement at the party.

Everyone went crazy and started applauding, as though the guy had just conducted a symphony or something. My mum couldn't believe her ears and strongly considered signing me up for violin classes right then and there.

The kid had just belted out DDLJ. What the fuck was wrong with everyone?

Which brings us back to the present day, when Chickoo has grown up to become Arjun and also the apple of his—and my—mother's eyes. So, many years later, I was once again en route to Anu Aunty's house for Arjun's birthday party. The moron was, for crying out loud, twenty-two-years old and still having such stupid kiddy parties. As expected, preparations had been made on a large scale by dear Anu Aunty. All of Arjun's certificates, 'Best Student', 'Best Employee' trophies, etc. etc. were on display in the living room.

The aunties couldn't stop gushing about what they saw.

'Look ya, working for InfoTech. Best employee also ya!' screamed one.

'I know. He always came first in school also no, Anu?' gushed another.

'I'm tho getting my Rupa married to him only', spoke a third with authority.

'Please Ritu, I've seen your Rupa's pictures on Facebook ya', retorted a particularly fat aunty.' 'Uff! her miniskirts get shorter by the day. You control her first and then think about her marriage.'

It was a glorious moment for Anu Aunty who was soaking it all in. The aunties were going crazy, wedding offers for Arjun had started pouring in, and had we waited for some more time,

I reckon a bidding war would have begun. It was as though Arjun was a desi rockstar and had this huge diehard 'Aunty' fan following, which couldn't get enough of him. It was the day Anu Aunty had waited for all her life and one that my mom had dreaded with equal fervour.

Though I tried my best to stay away from him, that sissy Arjun ran towards me.

'Hiii!' he shrieked like a sixteen-year-old girl.

'Hey man!' I gave him a manly handshake.

'So you still don't have a job yet ya?' he said, sounding eerily like his mother.

'Dude, don't you worry, when I get one you'll be the first to know.' I patted his shoulder and made my way to the dining table overflowing with delicacies. I filled my mouth with Hyderabadi biryani.

Meanwhile, Biju Uncle was busy stuffing my mum's ears and brain with future plans for me. Had we given him some more time, he would have even found a bride for me. As I was helping myself generously to the awesome paneer kofta, he caught me.

'So Varun, still no job, eh?' Aaargh, somebody kill me please.

'No uncle...uh...'

'Have you lost your mind, eh? Get a job. Look at Arjun, don't you want to be like him?'

Why the hell would any self-respecting twenty-two-year-old on this planet want to be like frickin' Arjun?

'Umm, uncle, I was thinking of starting something of my own,' I blurted out.

'What? Chee! Get these thoughts out of your brain,' Biju Uncle spat his words out. 'Why you want all this? Look at so many MNCs in Bangalore. Not only wonderful salaries they are giving, they are also giving perks.'

Wow. I pity anyone who is trying to start their own company if they have a dad like him.

'Uncle, but I don't *want* to do what everyone is doing.'

'Varun, you are disappointing. No job, then no MBA, and if no MBA, then no wife, and if no wife, then no dowry. What you going to do?'

Mother Swear

Another week went by. My joblessness had become the talk of the town and the aunties wanted to know if I would run some errands for them. Mum started giving me more 'responsible' jobs of buying groceries, and sometimes even letting me watch her cooking. One day, a lady came to visit my mum and she brought her eight-year-old son along with her. While they got busy in their conversation, I was entrusted with the tough job of 'babysitting' this kid. No amount of games or chocolates could bribe him to become my friend.

Eventually he did come around when I let him have the TV remote. I stepped out for a bit and came back to see the remote broken on the floor. I asked the kid what had happened and he said he knew nothing about it. I questioned him again but then he said something that took me back to a cozy corner in time: 'Mother Swear'.

I was reminded of all those words we used in school which were completely forgotten now. The usual classics were 'got jacked', 'sidey', 'fatty bomballaty', 'sorry won't make a dead man alive' and so on. Yet, 'mother swear' was definitely the most popular of them all. I mean there was always 'God promise', but nothing could beat the power of mother swear.

I remember how everyone would use it with the teachers and get away with it, every single time. When mother swear was in its heyday, all of us knew that the kid who had pinched his throat and said 'mother swear' was speaking the truth, no matter how heinous his crime, and was thus declared innocent. However, the teachers eventually found out that mother swear was a big scam and a valuable weapon was thus lost. I have vivid recollections of an incident in school when a classmate of mine was accused of throwing stink bombs in class. He was brought in front of the entire class and questioned.

'What men, throwing stink bombs in class and all. You're going to see the principal now,' the teacher said.

'But Miss, I never did it,' whimpered the boy.

'How do I believe you, men?'

'Miss...mother swear' The whole class went silent. He had used the holy words.

No one knows if he had actually thrown the stink bomb or not but he definitely set a trend.

Ah! How I miss those days. It's the mother of all swears—Mother Swear.

'Screw It, Let's Do It'

When you're jobless, the pace of time becomes very slow. Like excruciatingly slow. I was getting more and more addicted to Facebook and that had become a serious problem. During those days, Farmville was at its peak and people were going crazy sending each other pigs, horses, dogs and what not.

Devika had changed her profile picture to an even prettier one and I still couldn't figure out how to add her as my friend without her thinking of me as a creep. I was checking the comments on her pictures. It is funny how women just can't get enough of praising each other. I mean they post comments such as 'gorgeous', 'so pwetty', 'omg you look so pretty', and how can one forget, 'hotness?' For girls, it's almost like a ritual where if one of them uploads a new 'pic' of herself, it is mandatory for her friends to comment on it; even if the girl in question is not looking that 'pwetty'. What is even more weird is a girl 'marrying' another girl on Facebook. (That happens a lot, trust me!)

Apart from reflecting on the follies of man—and particularly womankind through Facebook, I had created a rough plan of the business idea during my jobless days and was desperate to get Mal involved to set the ball rolling. Luckily, Mal was now done with his project and was even more enthusiastic than me about it. So we decided to meet at Shiva's again that night to brainstorm.

We got to Shiva's at around 9 p.m. The waiters brought us plates of spicy hot masala dosas with an incredible chutney to go along with it. Bangalore's masala dosas are one of the best things on earth. If you haven't already fallen in love with its weather, its people, its pubs, its music, its 'adjust and chill maadi' culture and everything else that makes the city rock, then there is always its out-of-the-world masala dosa to keep you there.

Mal seemed agitated. I guess he too (like the rest of the world) was feeling the monotony and pressure of the 9 to 5 rut. Both us were now more determined than ever to get our endeavour off the ground.

Okay, so what did we have to do first? Well, if we were going to be a merchandise company, we needed to have the merchandise in place! The first things on our mind were the hoodies and T-shirts. So we had to find a suitable manufacturer who could make these for us and more importantly, give us the quality we wanted. Ideally, people would have done market research, drawn out charts, come up with possible numbers and filled up excel sheet upon excel sheet. But Mal and I didn't want to waste our time on any of that. We had seen too many people come up with great ideas and get stuck in the whirlpool of numbers, never venturing far enough to start their companies.

Thus, we decided to just take off and for this we needed to:

a) Find a suitable manufacturer since that was going to form the very crux of this business.

b) Find a suitable market or an event to test our business idea and our product.

Opportunity presented itself in the form of the Old Boys' day at our alma mater, Bishop Cotton Boys' School, which was to be held soon. It would be a perfect place to test out our business idea. Ex-Cottonians would be present there (we called ourselves Cottonians) and it would be great to see how they reacted to the merchandise we had planned. So we had a perfect market to test our idea but we still didn't have a manufacturer in place who could make us some samples. So Mal and I got into our usual discussion.

'Dude, the Cottonian reunion is happening on 29 June. This could be a perfect place for us to start.'

'Yeah dude I know. But we need to get samples made.' Mal said.

'Do you know of any manufacturers?' I enquired.

'I'm not sure man. We'll have to look.'

So that is what was decided in our first-ever business meeting. Well, our first-ever *official* business meeting. From that day on, both Mal and I started looking for manufacturers.

The next morning we got a few contacts from Justdial and we finally locked down a few local vendors. We called all of them up and set up meetings.

Our first stop was Sri Raju Textiles. His factory was as shady as the name of his company. It was this shabby little joint and it looked like someone had stuffed fifty workers in a pigeonhole. He had no office to speak of, so we conducted our meeting in one of the sheds. He offered us some sugarcane juice which I curtly said no to. Mal seemed to have enjoyed his drink and my only worry was that he should not end up dying on me.

We began the talks by first checking the quality of his products. He gave us a couple of sample tees which were equally shady.

'Saar, this is best quality,' he said spitting his paan out.

'Boss, do you have better quality than this?'

'Saar, people anly laving this quality, Saar.'

'Boss, we can't accept this quality; if you have anything better we can look.'

'Not possible Saar. But if you give advance money I give quality.'

'Why do you need advance, boss?'

'I buy good fabric Saar.'

'How much money you want?'

'Two lakh Saar. Only cash.'

The moment he said that, we were out of the place and already on our way to the next vendor. The next guy on our list was Om Fashions who was supposedly a big vendor. When we finally reached his factory we were actually impressed. This could be our guy, we thought. We had to wait for a good two hours before we were actually allowed to see the owner. He was an elderly man in his sixties and was clearly not impressed on seeing us.

'Rohn and Varun, you guys seemed older on the phone.' He said, clearly indicating his displeasure.

'Oh Sir, we only look young,' Mal said. I didn't know what he meant by that.

'So I like your idea boys.'

'Thank you, Sir.'

'So, what's the deal here? Who's investing in this? How many pieces will you be ordering every month? Should I be doing the printing also? How many colours are we looking at?

'Sir, we are not looking for anything big right now,' we said.

'What, then why have you come here?' His tone was getting curt.

'We first want some samples made and test them out at an event that's happening...'

He cut us off, 'Boys, I'm not a tailor. I don't make samples just like that. You have to buy a minimum of seven hundred pieces from me in each colour. That's an investment of ₹12 lakh. Do you have that much money?'

And with that we struck off Om Fashions as well. The third vendor didn't even have a factory of his own so we had to strike him off as well. Mal and I were spent and dejected. So much for our little business idea.

Meanwhile, Anu Aunty and my mum were scheming to get me a job. While both of them knew I detested working for a tech company, I could make out from the umpteen phone conversation that something was fishy.

The next night I got a text from Mal. 'Bro, meet me at Shiva's in half an hour. It's urgent.'

I landed at Shiva's where Mal was waiting with some good news.

'Bro, I have this family friend of mine in Tirupur, dude. I think we can go and talk to him. He makes stuff for all the big brands,' Mal said with Shiva and his boys constantly trying to overhear our conversation. I suspected they wanted to start the same business on their own.

'Dude, are you serious?'

'Yeah man, my dad told me about him, we have to go see him.'

'So we have to go to Tirupur.'

'Yup.'

'But where is it?'

'Let's find out.'

Before Shiva could hear anymore and get his own business going, it was decided that we would catch the train to Tirupur that weekend. The time for planning was over and even though we actually had no plan in place we had to get this thing started somewhere and going to Tirupur seemed like a wonderful place to start. In Richard Branson's own words, 'when you want to start something you just have to go out there and do it. There's no point thinking about it.' And as he very famously said 'SCREW IT, LET'S DO IT.'

Richard Branson is a very successful entrepreneur and founder of the Virgin group. His book *Losing My Virginity: The Autobiography* is highly recommended!

The T-shirt Capital of India

Until then I hadn't even heard of Tirupur. On googling the same, I found that it was the T-shirt capital of India. If T-shirts were being made in India, they were most likely being made in Tirupur.

So, our manufacturer was definitely in the right place. I was extremely happy that our idea was finally heading somewhere but what I didn't know was that my mum and Anu Aunty had other plans. It was a Thursday and I was about to leave the house to pick up the train tickets for Tirupur when Anu Aunty walked into the house.

These aunties don't have any job other than to go to other aunties' houses and bloody gossip.

'Varoon. Hi! Why in such a hurry ya? Where you going?'

'Aunty, I was just going out to...'

'Arre no. Wait ya, I have to talk to you.'

OH FUCK. THIS CAN'T BE GOOD.

My mum joined the festivities and I still couldn't understand what this was about.

'Achha, so I have good news for you.'

GOOD NEWS? WTF??

'We've found a job for you.'

'Job? But aunty, I don't want a job.'

'What do you mean, Varun? You don't want to work ever?' My mum barged in as though I had just told her I never want to marry.

'Uh mom, but I need a little time.'

'What time? You're only sleeping all day. Have you seen Jignesh uncle's son. He is a manager now at Wipro. You used to play cricket with that boy. And with that she shed the token tear which every Indian mother does at this point.

In India, it is a ritual that if one lady cries, any other lady present near her has to show solidarity by crying with her. Thus, when my mum unleashed the first few droplets, Anu Aunty's eyes got wet as well.

I was wondering if I should tell them about my 'idea'. But then, common sense prevailed. If I was to tell them my idea there would be such a huge backlash from both of them that I would have to spend the rest of my life working in a call centre. Also, luckily for me, Neelu aunty walked in which gave me an opportunity to run out. As I was leaving, I could see the three of them engaged in a group crying session.

Now the last thing any young entrepreneur in India should do is share his business idea with his parents. The parents will first listen to the idea and then give you a million reasons for why you would fail and absolutely never endorse it. So if you're thinking of sticking it out on your own, never ever tell your parents. Trust me.

The Journey Begins

Our train was due to leave at 10.15 p.m. the following Friday night. Now both Mal and I have the distinction of reaching ridiculously late anywhere we go, and this particular instance was no different. We reached the station five minutes before the train was scheduled to leave and we were struggling to find the platform where it left from. While we were still on the bridge, one of us asked a bystander which platform the train to Tirupur was leaving from. He pointed to a moving train below us.

Damn.

The scene was exactly like the last scene of DDLJ except that in this case, both of us were outside the train and running towards it. Mal threw in both our bags in one boogie and got into the next one. I managed to get into the neighbouring boogie. Therefore, Mal, our bags and I were all in different boogies. We finally assembled near our seats only to find someone else sitting there. And that's when the harsh truth dawned on us. Our tickets had not been confirmed! We had to stand all the way on this ten-hour-long journey.

We eventually found a TC by the name of Mr Sivamani and tried pleading with him.

'Sir, our seats are not confirmed. Can you please do something?'

His evil laugh confirmed our worst fears.

'No seat pa. Only standing. He he...'

No amount of bribe would pacify the bearded monster. There was no way he was giving us any seats and he seemed to be getting some really sick pleasure out of all this. I've always had bad luck with train tickets all my life and have always met demons like Mr Sivamani who have made it even more difficult.

By the time we reached Tirupur, we were in pain. Real, tangible pain.

Tirupur reminded me of the ghost town in *Jab We Met*. Deserted streets, dingy hotels and complete darkness. We landed up in a shady hotel with the receptionist digging his nose furiously. We were on a very strict budget so there was no money for any opulence. We freshened up quickly and were on our way to meet 'the manufacturer'.

Meeting Purshottam, our manufacturer, was the only good thing that had happened so far. We were extremely impressed by his factory and clearly, he had been working for some really big international brands. He happened to be a family friend of Mal's and that is why he had agreed to even meet us.

For any young entrepreneur who lands up in Tirupur, finding a manufacturer is not tough. But finding the right one is extremely difficult. This town is known for duping retailers, and luckily, we had found someone we knew. So all you guys planning to go down that road, please do a thorough check in case you're meeting any manufacturers in Tirupur.

Luckily for us, Purshottam was more or less our age. He had taken over from his dad and, more importantly, he understood our concept. We explained the entire idea to him and how we intended to take this further. He didn't seem too impressed at first but he liked our enthusiasm. So basically, this was the deal we cut with him. He agreed to make the samples for us for free provided we placed a big order with him. If we failed to do so, we'd have to pay—not only for the samples but also for the fabric which amounted to around ₹4 lakh. So here we were on the brink of a major decision. If we told him 'Yes' we stood a chance of losing ₹4 lakh (which we clearly didn't have) and if we said 'No' we went back to our insignificant lives.

This was a far cry from our first meeting at Noon Wines. It is usually very easy to talk about ideas and discuss them and feel all good about it. But it's moments like these which make everything real. It's moments like these when you can no longer be a kid or a wannabe entrepreneur.

I don't think we actually thought about anything. The word YES came out from both our mouths in less than thirty seconds. 'SCREW IT, LET'S DO IT', remember? We had to do this and if it meant working in our dear manufacturer's factory to pay him, we were going to do it.

We were on top of the world on our way back. We had a lavish meal and downed some beers. Our little company was finally taking shape. Now that we had samples and someone to produce them in place, we started thinking of all kinds of names for our company. Two of the names we thought of were 'Lemontee' and 'Backbenchers'. But both of us really loved Backbenchers. We thought it was young, brash and more importantly, it was who we were. We reached Bangalore early next morning. Now we not only had a name for the company, but we also had samples coming in in a week's time. Finally, the realization of that little idea born in Noon Wines was in sight. At least for now.

Business Lessons from Aunties

Back at home, things were exactly where I had left them. My mum had no clue what I was upto and Anu Aunty was still conspiring to get me a job. Mum was now moving me into greater responsibilities and had taken it upon herself to teach me how to buy groceries.

We landed at the grocery store and the vendors alerted each other on seeing my mum. They threw off their smokes, stopped lazing around and got ready for the duel.

'How much for the onions?' Mum asked an innocent looking vegetable vendor.

'Twenty rupees, madam. But for you fifteen rupees,' he said with his hands trembling.

'Joking or what? Pack two kgs for eight rupees,' she said triumphantly.

'But madam...'

Before the poor guy could say anything else, mum had moved on to the fruit vendor.

'Apples for how much?'

'Only twenty rupees madam.'

'What??'

'He he, yes madam.'

'Pack if for twelve. Not a rupee more.'

'But madam...'

After successfully killing every vendor in sight we finally got to the auto stand to go back.

'Koramangala,' my mum said.

'Handred rupees,' the auto guy replied cockily.

The next thing I knew, my mum had complained to the nearest traffic constable who charged the poor soul with a considerable fine. We were now in his auto on our way to Koramangala for only twenty rupees.

As a kid, I would always get pissed when my aunt or mum bargained with the vegetable vendor or the auto guy or with every other person possible. I'm pretty sure most of you have been through this as well and have been well embarrassed by your mum or aunt trying to save even the last rupee on everything. In my younger days, I always thought this was unnecessary, but now that I was about to start my own business, I realized that I wasn't paying close attention.

You see, the aunties of India have mastered the fine art of negotiation and could easily give Donald Trump a run for his money. I think the greatest MBA school is observing your mum or aunt haggle with the vegetable vendor and trying to learn and teach the tricks of the trade. Not only do they get the guy to sell the onions at a far lesser price, they convince him that he has made money (which he has clearly not).

The greatest skill any entrepreneur should acquire is the art of negotiation. And to learn this art you don't need any business school. Refer to the nearest aunty around you and observe her closely. If you can implement even 10 per cent of the mojo with which she bargains and implement that in your business, you'll be hitting your first million in no time!

So the next time you overhear any aunty saying, 'That and all is okay but how much discount will you give?'—pay attention. Pay very close attention.

Anu Aunty Strikes

The day our shipment carrying the samples was to arrive was drawing near. The Old Boys' Day at Bishop Cotton was on 29 June and we had to get permission from the principal and the alumni association to set the ball rolling. Without their permission, there was no way we could set up a stall and display our samples. The principal during our time in school had moved on so we had to start from scratch, but the fact that we were old boys could work in our favour.

Every entrepreneur has to go through the 'pitch'. That is what determines everything. 'Pitch' is basically how well you sell your idea and convince the other person about it. We had taken an appointment to meet him but had to wait for the samples because there wouldn't be any point meeting him without showing him the product we were trying to sell.

Meanwhile, things at home were getting a little uneasy for me. Anu Aunty had fixed a job interview for me on Friday afternoon. This was, of course, exactly the same day the principal of Bishop Cotton had given us an appointment for.

This got me into a terrible fix. I definitely had no intention of going for the interview but I also didn't want my family, and especially Anu Aunty, to find out what I was up to.

It was Wednesday and I was awakened early in the morning by my landline ringing constantly. This was extremely strange since nobody calls on a landline these days. So I answered the phone, and on the other line was a lady with a familiar-sounding voice.

'Hellooo, could I speak with Poornima, please?' she said.

'May I know who is calling?' I said.

'It's Anu here.' My hands started trembling.

(Oh Fuck!)

(Awkward Silence)

'Varun, is that you?'

(Awkward Silence)

'Oh! Anu Aunty? Hello, aunty,' I said, bringing all the fake pleasantness and courtesy I could gather into my voice.

(Awkward Silence)

'Varooon, I hope you haven't forgotten about Friday ya. You have that interview and you cannot bunk it, OK?'

(Awkward Silence)

'Ah…umm…where is it, aunty? I might have some work,' I said.

'Oh c'mon Varun, what work? Your mother tells me you sleep all day, you have to go.'

'Sleep all day? No, aunty, I'm working on something.'

'No, Varun. I know everything. Even Biju Uncle is going to be there. He wants to talk to you.'

'Uh, aunty...but...'

'No but git n' all, Varun. Now please give the phone to Poornima, no.'

Damn! I had to get out of this and I had to come up with an excuse very soon.

The boys decided to meet up for a mid-week drink that day and we found ourselves holed up in Satya's Bar and Restaurant. Satya's was like any other bar and restaurant in India. The funny thing about these places is that no one usually eats in such places. All the boys were in attendance, save for Mal, who had excused himself due to overload of work at KGMP. I was really keen on getting drunk as quickly as possible. Anu Aunty had put way too much pressure on me and I was way too stressed.

The first round of Blender's Pride was gulped down in an instant.

'So Varun, tell us da, what's happening with Devika?' asked Sid.

'Ooooo!' All of them howled in unison.

'Still haven't added her guys,' I said.

'What, are you fucking serious?' Sid tends to get really aggressive when he is drunk.

'You're such a pussy,' yelled Mehta.

This coming from a guy who was twenty-four and had never kissed a girl.

Drinks were now flowing and everyone was a little tight. Sid was getting angrier while Rohit and Mehtu were engaged in a serious discussion on the subprime crisis.

'I fucking hate this country and hate this system. There are no fucking jobs for someone like me. *Me*, I bloody graduated from LSE!' Sid banged his fist on the table.

'So? What's the big deal in graduating from LSE, man? Every Tom, Dick and Harry is from there these days,' Rohit pitched in, adding fuel to the fire.

'What the hell is wrong with you, fuckface? Not everyone can get into LSE,' said Sid.

'Who the fuck are you calling fuckface, you slut,' said Rohit.

'Aye Bob, chill out Bob,' Mehta butted in trying to resolve the matter.

'Mehtu, you fucking stay out this, you shit,' Sid screamed loud enough to draw the attention of the manager.

'You're such a pussy, da Sid,' said Mehtu.

'Pussy? Who the hell are you calling a pussy, you bastard?'

I am usually very calm when I'm drunk but there was a lot on my mind that night. So I did something completely unexpected. I stood up and started shouting at them.

'Guys, you fucking idiots, look at yourselves fighting over stupid shit. All of you are pussies and all of you are bastards. Sid, if you're so desperate for a job why don't you create one man? That's right. No one in this country wants to take any risks. Everyone wants a happy-go-lucky MNC job, all the perks in the world and the weekend off. Even if you're sitting on the bench in the company, it doesn't matter as long as you have a job, right?

'If everyone starts thinking this way, how the hell will this country have any entrepreneurs or anything else man? Imagine, if in the 80s, Narayana Murthy had thought, "Why the hell am I not getting a job?" Who would have given jobs to asses like you all today? Why the hell is everyone so foolishly limited to a single track when it comes to this? Why does everyone have to follow the plan? First, you're expected to get good grades, then you're expected to get into a good college, then you're expected to get into a company and then get an MBA—this is such a load of shit!

'How will anyone do what they want to do here? If you want to become a filmmaker, you're laughed at; if you want to start your own company, you're laughed at. Rohit, you stupid fuck, look at you. You were one of the finest cricketers around when we were in school. You could have done such great things, but look at you—living your life in fear and still struggling with your GMAT. And Gujju Boy, you, you're one of the greatest designers I have ever seen. You can sketch and draw man, and that's such a great fucking talent, and look at you dreaming of going to USA and becoming a techie. You know what's the funny part? When you're done living someone else's dream and you are old and depressed, all of you will think about this day and say "WHY THE FUCK DID I DO WHAT EVERYONE ELSE WANTED ME TO DO?"'

Silence.

Even the waiters had stopped serving. Everyone was looking at me as though I had just given an Oscar speech or something. No one even batted an eyelid. The boys were absolutely stunned as was the rest of the crowd. I was expecting everyone to burst into applause anytime now. And right then Sid burst into 'Kajarare' and was promptly joined in by Rohit and Gujju Boy. There were no claps, no salutations, nothing. And with that, everything I said was completely forgotten.

BackBenchers Inc.?

I woke up early the next morning. My mother was completely shocked and duly called up all her kitty party friends to inform them of the miracle. I was obviously extremely excited and couldn't sleep much. The samples were coming in today and we were going to take these and show them to the principal the next day.

The samples were due to come in at five in the evening. Mal had left work earlier that day and had come straight to my house. Mum was wondering what was going on, and thankfully the cunning Anu Aunty was missing in action.

It was now 5.30 p.m. and still no signs of the package. We started calling the courier people desperately to track it. We finally managed to squeeze out the driver's number from them but his phone was not reachable. It was now around 8.30 p.m. and we were getting really worried. If we didn't have the samples by today we couldn't meet with the principal the next day and the entire plan was virtually off. What made matters worse was the fact that we had ₹4 lakh riding on this and if this didn't work out, we would be slaves to the manufacturer for a few days and would probably have to do a stint in his factory to pay off our debts.

While all these thoughts were cramping in my head, my phone was constantly ringing. It was Anu Aunty and she was calling to confirm the interview for the next day. I was in half a mind to kill someone and if the samples were not going to show up on time, I could only picture myself becoming junior Arjun.

Mal and I were frantically calling the courier guys every two minutes but it was now a lost cause. Not only were they not taking our calls but it had started to pour heavily. This was almost the end. Just the thought of picturing ourselves slogging it out at the factory for a few months made me panic. But we weren't going to go down so easily and thus, we decided to walk into the courier company's office and demand for our courier. We landed up there but they said the same thing that they had been trying to say all this while. The driver who had our box was not reachable and till he came back, we had no option at all. So we decided to do what anyone else in our situation would do. WAIT.

And wait we did. We must have waited for two hours when the office manager informed us that the driver may have been stuck somewhere because of the rains. We asked him what time could we expect the delivery the next day. He said '11.00 a.m.' Our appointment with the principal was at 11.00 a.m.

I couldn't get any sleep that night. All kinds of weird thoughts filled my head—Anu Aunty, our samples, that sissy

Arjun, Devika's profile picture and more importantly, the question—what was I doing with my life? I was beginning to feel that maybe everyone was right. Maybe this wasn't meant to be. Maybe I should just get a job. Maybe one really can't pursue something of their own in this country. Maybe this is the end. Maybe I should forget the whole fucking thing. Anu Aunty's words 'No MBA, no future' kept ringing in my head.

'Here Comes the Sun'

'Barun bhaiya, Barun bhaiya!'

It was eight in the morning. I was wondering what the hell could Lalit want from me at this hour? I looked up at him with my eyes half open. All I could see was Lalit holding a big parcel. I got up in an instant. The courier guy! He was here. Shit. I ran towards the door, signed the necessary papers and arranged all the boxes in the hall. I recited a small prayer and opened the box.

Wow.

There are some moments in life that cannot be described in words. This definitely was one of those moments. I was actually holding our 'idea' right there in my hands and I can tell you, it was the greatest feeling ever. Oh! it looked awesome. If I was an alumnus of Bishop Cotton I would want one of those. Mal was at my place in an instant and even he was overwhelmed with what he saw.

We had our meeting at eleven but in the entire process we had forgotten to print our business cards. Our very own business cards! One of the greatest joys in starting your company is getting your business cards printed. It gives you this great feeling of accomplishment. We were on our way to Print Xpress when something happened.

'Mal, are you sure you want to go with BackBenchers?' I asked.

'Yeah dude, why not, I think it's cool,' Mal said.

'Dude, remember that other name you had come up with?'

'Which one?'

'Alma Mater.'

'Alma Mater? I'm not too sure of that, dude.'

'Dude, we would be dealing with principals and heads of institutions. I don't think Backbenchers would hit the right note, don't you think?'

'Hmmm.'

After we reached Print Xpress we got new business cards made. We were now Alma Mater. Officially.

Alma Mater refers to a school, college, or university attended during one's formative years and the name described our company perfectly. But yeah, I know, Backbenchers was the shit. We had copyrighted the name though, so if any of you enthusiasts are trying to start your own company with the name Backbenchers, watch out.

I was going back to school after five long years. It was a wonderful experience. Bishop Cotton Boys' School, Bangalore was founded in 1865 and is one of the oldest and most prestigious institutions in this country. The list of achievers that this school has produced is endless.

We went straight to the principal's office and this was it—our first ever pitch. We told him about our idea, our company and finally showed him the samples. He was mighty impressed and added that he had absolutely no issues with us coming on the Old Boys' Day to display and sell the merchandise as long as the OCA (Old Cottonian's Association) was informed and we obtained the necessary permissions from them. We then handed him our business cards and parted ways. Phew, our first ever business meeting and it felt so bloody good.

I'm telling you one thing guys, starting your own company is super fun. Don't ever pass on that. Because after that first business meeting, a whole new rush of self-confidence flows into you.

We immediately got in touch with the alumni association and told them about the entire plan. They were not only happy but were very supportive.

One of the association members even commented, 'I'm glad the youngsters are doing all this. This will only strengthen the alumni association.'

We signed a letter with them, giving them a royalty on every product sold. We also outlined the products and a number of other clauses like payment schedule, timelines etc.

Once the association signed the letter, we were officially in business. In a day's time, we had chosen a name for our company, got business cards made, made our first pitch and signed our first agreement. The day couldn't have gotten any better.

But things at home were going horribly wrong again. I had bunked my interview without informing anyone and when I reached home it wasn't the prettiest of sights. Anu Aunty and my mum were waiting for me and what's worse, an army of other aunties had joined them. This was definitely not a good sign. I was in for some serious trouble and as the Bangaloreans would have it—I was gone for a toss. It was a completely hopeless situation.

Anu Aunty was the ringleader of these aunties. All of them, including my mum, listened to what she said and her word was final. Even Neelu aunty, who was quite fond of me, didn't have the audacity to talk in front of Anu Aunty. I was screwed and how. The aunties were deep in gossip when I walked in. All of them were giving me dirty looks as if I had hacked into their Facebook accounts or something. I pretended to be completely ignorant but that didn't work. These aunties are way smarter and sooner or later they will get you.

'So Varun, what happened today?' Rupa aunty began the proceedings.

'Umm, oh aunty...uh I had some work,' I said.

'What work, man? All day long you're lazing around n all...your mother says,' I was surprised Pinto aunty got the opportunity to speak because she wasn't part of Anu Aunty's core group.

'Uh no aunty, actually, I...'

My mum barged in with the token tear in her eye. 'Varun, why can't you just listen to Anu Aunty? You are always doing what you want, never listening to me. At least do what she says.'

Shit, it's going to be a crying session again.

'Varoon, you tell me one thing ya, if you behave like this, which girl will marry you?' Kitty aunty butted in.

Why the hell do these aunties know nothing except marriage? Is that the sole purpose of our existence?

'But I don't want to get a job.' I screamed. Absolute silence followed. The aunties couldn't believe their ears, as though I had just converted to another religion. And that's when Anu Aunty finally spoke.

'Varoooon. If you are snoozing you are losing,' she said with finality.

And all the other ladies started applauding Anu Aunty. I couldn't believe this. Firstly, she had just murdered a very famous proverb and on top of that, the other aunties were going gaga over her supposedly smart quip.

'Varun, Anu and I have decided you will be seeing a counsellor soon. That's the only way you will figure out what to do with your life,' my mum said.

'You can go now, Varoon. But don't forget my words,' said Anu Aunty menacingly.

And just like that I was dismissed. As I was leaving, I could see Anu Aunty perched on the sofa like a queen with the other aunties surrounding her like minions. Man, what was the world coming to?

Part 2

'How Much for this Hoodie, Bro?'

The D-day had finally arrived. It was 29 June—the Old Cottonians' day. We were all set to go. Fresh cards had been printed, order books were packed, we got a nice little banner made and were finally ready. This was the moment of truth for us. I had already been reading up on a life of a factory worker just in case things didn't work out.

Both Mal and I wore our sweatshirts or hoodies. Students from Bishop Cotton were called Cottonians and we had these nice bottle-green hoodies made which said COTTONIAN in bold. This was our flagship product. Yes, you guessed it right. Like those Harvard and Stanford hoodies. Our products looked good and we were hoping that the others would find them appealing too.

We stuffed all the samples and other paraphernalia in Mal's dad's car and made our way to the school. We had certainly come a long way since our Noon Wines days and even if things didn't work out today, at least we would go down having given it a shot.

We reached school much before everything started and surprisingly, there was hardly anyone present. As we were getting out of the car and pulling the stuff out, a student currently studying there walked up to me.

'Hey man, are you an ex-student?' he asked.

'Yup, batch of 2004,' I said.

'Cool. That's a funny sweatshirt you're wearing.'

Oh fuck. Mal and I looked at each other. This can't be true. The present students don't like it? We thought they'd be lining up for this shit.

Anyway, we got all the stuff out and set up our little stall near the main building of the school. Then we waited. It was 10.00 a.m. and there was still some time before the Old Boys' breakfast got over. The school watchman was wandering nearby and caught a glimpse of our samples. Some teachers passed by but they seemed completely disinterested in what they saw. Some students were running around but they couldn't care less.

The breakfast finally got over and people slowly started emerging from the main hall. Not many saw our stall and whoever did, gave it a miss.

But then something happened. This junior of ours from school recognized me and walked up to me.

'Bro, wazzaa? Long time,' he said.

'Hey man!' I said.

'What you got here, bro?'

'Ah, some merchandise for the old boys.'

'Hey, nice hoodie, bro,' he said, picking up a grey hoodie.

'Thanks man,' I said.

'Bro, are you selling this by any chance?'

Though he could be our very first customer, his excessive use of 'bro' was annoying the shit out of me.

'Yeah man, that's why we are here.'

'Bro, this is fucking cool, bro.'

'You want one?'

'Yeah, bro. How much?'

'Five hundred dude.'

'Whoa...neat bro...okay, I gotta rush to the ATM bro. Save a Large size for me.'

And with that the enthu cutlet vanished. Our first 'potential' customer. No one even as much as walked up to our stall for the next hour. Our 'bro' too had failed to show up in spite of the ATM being across the street.

Ah! Fuck this shit, I thought. Let's get down to being a factory worker, at least I'll be away from Anu Aunty. I went to the loo in despair. While washing my hands, I looked at myself in the mirror and could not help but reflect on what a disappointment I had become. I had disappointed my friends, my parents and more importantly, myself. I felt really sick and wanted to go home right away. Again, Anu Aunty started dominating my thoughts and I kept thinking how happy she would be when she would hear that this little business of mine had failed.

I walked back to the stall and only one word, one that I use pretty regularly, could describe what came to my mind. FUCK.

You know, when you read about or hear people talking about miracles on TV, it sounds really funny. None of that stuff actually ever happens, right? But there are times when some of it really happens to you. It did to me.

There was this HUGE, HUGE crowd in front of our stall—it was massive. Our good friend 'bro' was there too with twenty other friends of his. Apparently, he had gone out and called every other old Cottonian and had told them about us. There were present Cottonians, old Cottonains and everyone wanted something. They were all calling their friends and their friends were calling other people, and telling them about 'Alma Mater'.

We had gotten only hundred business cards printed but they vanished in fifteen minutes. Soon we were writing our numbers on small chits of paper. We couldn't believe it. There was such a rush that I didn't even have the time to cry! People just couldn't get enough of our hoodies and tees. They were selling like hot cakes. We couldn't even find the time to eat. By the time we got done, it was six in the evening.

All our samples were sold. Even the hoodies we had been wearing were sold and we had to borrow T-shirts from the present boarders. But this was the good part—Can you imagine how many hoodies we booked in five hours? Sixteen hundred. Yes, thousand fucking six hundred.

Guys, if you do start a business of your own some day, a day like this will come. When it does, please come back and read the above chapter again. You will feel what I felt.

Phew. We did what seemed most logical at that time. We went to Noon Wines to celebrate.

That was one of the greatest days of my life.

The Adventures of Dr Swamy

I woke up the next morning with a splitting headache, but I was really happy. We were in the process of turning our first business idea into an actual business and just the thought of it got me super excited. But my happiness was short-lived.

Lalit hurried into my room. 'Bhaiya, get ready. Fast, mummy waiting.' *Waiting? Waiting for what?*

'Varun. Get ready in five minutes. We are meeting the counsellor today,' my mother said.

OH FUCK, NO! Here I am, the hotshot co-founder of a new start-up and my mum is taking me to see a counsellor.

The next thing I knew, we were driving down MG Road and were neck deep in traffic. One of the worst things about this city is the traffic and my mum had gotten a peak traffic hour appointment for me. She usually doesn't say much in the car she but was all talk that day.

'Hey Varun, you remember Sonu aunty's son Roopal?' she said.

Roopal. This guy is the biggest porn addict I've ever known.

'Yeah, what about him, mom?'

'He is going to the US now for studies, no.'

Wow. The first thing the kid is going to do when he lands there is go to a strip club.

'Accha, and you know what Bubbly's daughter Rinku is doing?'

Rinku. She used to make passes at me when we were in the eighth standard. She had more facial hair than me.

'No mom, I don't. And I don't really care,' I shouted, frustrated by the slow moving traffic.

'Arrey, listen no. She's doing her MBA in Mumbai.'

I hope she had started shaving.

The traffic situation was clearly not improving and I was completely trapped. If something didn't happen soon I would have to listen to what my mum's kitty party friends' kids were up to for the next half an hour. But just then I heard a familiar voice calling my mum's name from the neighbouring car. It was Sheila aunty.

Oh thank Jesus for this!

Sheila aunty and my mum have hated each other for ages now. She had this daughter who was just as good or rather just as bad in studies as me and our mothers would always fight over who was better.

This war for mediocrity was the most hilarious thing ever. I mean imagine them saying, 'My son got 71 per cent and your daughter got only 70. Take that, bitch.'

My mum ducked and forced me to follow suit. But Sheila aunty was way too observant for that. She could clearly see us. 'Poo. Hey ya,' she said excitedly.

Mum knew there was no way out now and replied with an extremely fake, 'Sheilaaaa. Long time!'

I can't understand why women do that. They have this strange talent that allows them to be insanely excited in an extremely fake way when they see the person they clearly hate.

Now both the ladies knew that time was running out. The signal could turn green any moment and the cars would have to move. So Sheila aunty got straight to what she actually wanted to know.

'So Varun, what are you doing these days?'

'Oh, aunty, I'm not doing...'

Before I could say anything more, I was cut off by my mum.

'Oh, Varun is going to USA ya for his MBA,' she said.

'Arre wah. So is Neha. How cool na.'

Oh Shit.

Before the ladies could find out who had managed to get a bigger ring from their husbands or who had learnt to cook the latest Italian dish, the signal turned green and we parted ways.

My mum didn't say a word after that through the entire journey. She couldn't, because Neha was going to the US to do an MBA and I was going to a counsellor.

As expected, we reached the counsellor's place twenty minutes late. It was this old colonial bungalow, but the place was pretty neatly done. For some strange reason, there was a poster on the wall which said: 'We two, our's one'. We took our place on the sofa and waited for our turn. The receptionist was the best thing about the place. She was actually hot. I mean really hot. I wanted to strike up a conversation with her and was wondering what the hell was she doing being a receptionist at Dr Swamy's Quality Counselling Centre. I couldn't help but wonder if the counsellor had a scene with her. 'Okay, you're next,' she said, chewing her gum which made her look even hotter.

We entered Dr Swamy's office which was filled with his pictures with various personalities and dignitaries. They looked really fake though. I still kept wondering if he had a scene with his receptionist.

He was a portly man of around forty I guess, with sandalwood paste across his head.

'Coume saan. So Madam, what is tha problem heere?' he said.

'Dr Swamy, my son Varun is very confused. He doesn't know what he wants in life.'

'Ah, typical case I see,' he said, leaning back on his swivelling chair.

'Uh, no Dr Swamy, actually...' I tried to intervene.

'He sleeps all day and goes out in the night. He doesn't want to do a job, nothing,' my mother butted in.

'Oho! Prablem is vary seerious, no?' Dr Swamy said.

'I don't know what to do, sir. Please help.'

And with that my mum unleashed her token tear which got even Dr Swamy emotional.

'Vaaron, whaat is this I say?' he said.

'Actually Dr Swamy, I know what I want to do and I have...' I began, only to be cut off again.

'Saan, Laat of kids coming these days with same problems. But there is naw need to waary. Are you on drags?' he asked.

On hearing this, mum started crying even louder.

Just when things were getting really fucked up, the receptionist walked in. She walked up straight to Dr Swamy and bent over him and showed him a note. Her cleavage was more than visible to everyone present and that confirmed my worst fears. Anyway, the note was a grand saviour because for some strange reason, Dr Swamy had to leave in a hurry with the receptionist. I was saved, at least for now.

Dummies' Guide to E-Commerce

Over the next few days we tabulated all the orders from the Old Boys' event. We had a good number of orders in our kitty and we knew Purshottam was going to be happy. Mal and I were meeting at Shiva's again, which had become our temporary company headquarters. We had threatened Shiva and his boys of legal consequences if they stole our idea, so we had no reason to worry anymore. The tabulated sheet was sent to Purshottam who proceeded to start the manufacturing process. But there was one serious question that still haunted us. While we were selling the merchandise on the Old Boys' Day, this one gentleman from the batch of '78 walked up to us and asked us a very simple question—'Boys, I live in San Francisco. If I wanna get hold of one these, how do I do that?'

That one single question got us thinking. Maybe our grand dream of opening retail stores all over the country was not the right thing to do. For one, it would need a lot of money and we didn't know where that would come from. And secondly, it would complicate the logistics. So then, both Mal and I came to a consensus. What we needed was an e-commerce store.

Shiva and his boys seemed to be taking notes while we discussed all this and would immediately put their pens down when we looked at them in spite of our warnings.

Not only was an e-commerce store more affordable but it was more practical too. I mean, think of it, through an e-commerce store, anyone in the world who wanted to buy any of our products could do so. Now compare this to having an actual physical store somewhere.

Firstly, there would be very high rental costs. Secondly, we would need a full-time person to take care of it. Thirdly, it would cater to customers only around that area. An e-commerce store on the other hand is free of all these issues and moreover, anyone from anywhere in the world could be our customer. All you needed was a credit card and the courier companies had now even come up with the 'Cash on Delivery' offer so you could also pay once you received your goods. So the next logical step to take our company forward was to start an e-commerce website. Luckily for us, Mal's brother owned a company called Exit Designs that dealt with designing and developing websites apart from a host of other things. So we set up a meeting with him for three days later.

Dad's Business

It was Saturday night and we had been invited to Sahil's party. He was an old friend of ours and had called us stags for his birthday.

A stag is a single Indian male who usually goes to night clubs on weekends with other singles males with just one goal. To hit on women. He is usually not successful, so he repeats the process again on the next weekend.

The party was in a happening club in Bangalore called Hint. It had a huge dance floor, and a crazy-ass bar. The best part about this club was the awesome balcony overlooking the entire city.

We were four stags and had to get to the place by nine. The sad thing about this city is that it shuts down at 11.30 p.m., so even if it sounds really nerdy, one had to get to a party by 9.30 p.m. at least. The guest list was open only till nine and there was absolutely no stag entry after that. But then again, it was us. There was no way we were making it there by nine.

We had gone pre-drinking to Satya's because nobody would have the money to buy booze inside. I've always hated the concept of stag entry. How do these clubs expect boys to show up with girls all the time? And in India, only forty to fifty out of every hundred girls party, right? Out of these, at least twenty-five will have boyfriends and remaining will tag along with their friends who already have boyfriends. So stags like us have absolutely no chance of getting a couple entry. To make things worse, they expect the guys to show up by nine.

We finished our pre-drinking and landed there by nine-thirty. We walked in and were duly stopped at the entrance by a bouncer. Sid was way too drunk and started pretending to talk like an African-American and that irritated the shit out of us.

'Sir, you can't enter here as a stag,' the bouncer informed us.

'Oh yes, we can, nigga. We got no bitches but we enterin' this joint,' Sid's tone pissed the bouncer off.

'Sir, please watch your language,' he said.

'Do you know who you talkin to mothafucka? You ain't gonna stop me,' said Sid.

'Sir, please.'

'What you gonna do, N-I-GG-AA?'

And with that, the entire episode ended. First Sid went flying, then Rohit, then Mehtu and finally me.

We collected ourselves at the door and did the walk of shame. Luckily, no one saw. We were about to leave when Sahil finally emerged from Hint.

'Boys, wazz the sceeeeene? Where were you guys?' he asked.

'Dude, we got late man,' I said hastily, before others could speak.

'No worrizzz. Party at my place, daa. This place sucks.'

An hour later we found ourselves at Sahil's place, rather palace. Sahil's dad was into real estate and the guy was pretty loaded, driving in a BMW, et al. The house had a massive driveway, high ceilings, a gorgeous stairway and above all, one of the sexiest pools I have ever seen. The party was happening near the pool and some insanely hot girls were inside it. Our Gujju Boy had never seen so many women in a bikini at the same place. We settled ourselves near the bar like four losers ogling at every girl who walked past us. If only Sid didn't get us into trouble again, we had a half decent chance to get lucky. Okay fine, maybe not lucky but at least we had a chance to talk to some girls.

'Boys, where'z your drinks, raa?' Sahil shouted from the other end of the pool.

The bartender served up four Blue Labels in an instant. Yup, when you're in Sahil's house you not only drink the best, but you also get the best royal treatment.

We met a lot of school friends that night. Boys we hadn't seen for a long time. There was Rahul who met us first.

'Rahul, how's it going, man?' we asked.

'All cool, boys,' he said.

'What you upto these days, man?'

'Dad's business, boys.'

Then came Vasu.

'Vasu, what's going on man?' we asked.

'Dude, helping my dad with his business, dude,' he said.

Then came Rohan, Abhishek, Nikhil, Ajit and a host of others. All had only one thing to say—'Dad's business, bro.'

I guess in no other country does this phenomenon exist. You educate the kid, make him get a 'phoren' degree and then you make him join 'Dad's Business'. No wonder we have a shortage of both ideas and entrepreneurs in this country. That's because half of them are doing 'Dad's Business' and the other half working for some tech company.

I knew that if I stood there drinking with the three musketeers, there was no way I was meeting any girls that night. That's because even if one of us as much as talked to a girl, the others would go 'Oooooo' repelling them so far away that they never came back. So I took my drink and walked around. I ran into Arpita, a friend of mine from tuition. You see, I had done engineering and when you're pursuing this particular branch of studies, the number of women you know is usually below ten, or maybe even less. Out of these, the hot ones are usually one or two and that too only if you're lucky.

Surprisingly, Arpita had suddenly turned pretty, much to my disbelief. I never knew her eyes were hazel brown.

What do these women do? I mean they look all dorky with braces and stuff in school and then when you meet them a few years later they blow your mind away.

'Varun, hey, long time,' she said.

'Arpita, wow. It's been ages, really. How have you been?'

I was trying my best to conceal the fact that I thought she was smoking hot.

'Been good ya, and you?'

'Same old, Arpita. So what you up to these days?'

'I'm helping my dad with his business,' she said matter-of-factly.

WAIT. WHAT??? WTF???

But it didn't matter, did it? She was hot.

'Oh that's great, Arpita. Dad's business is really great. It's been so long, we should meet for coffee sometime, no?'

Women sense desperation. They have this sixth sense or something and they know when a guy is trying too hard.

'Uhm yeah. Oh Varun, have you met my boyfriend Vinay?' she said, pointing to a hunk who emerged from nowhere.

See, I told you.

'Oh! Hey Vinay, how is it going?' I said.

'Hey nice to meet you, bud,' said Vinay, shaking my hand.

'Nice party, haan?'

I sucked at small talk.

'True that.'

'So, what do you do?'

'Ah, I just joined my dad's business, bud,' said Vinay.

I ran back to my boys, who by now were in some very serious trouble. Sid, as usual, had got into a mess and a fight was about to begin.

'You fucking pussy, stop hiding,' he said. I think the word pussy can be patented or something by Sid.

'You bastard, I'll kill you.' That was Rohit. Yep, they come to a party and instead of fighting with someone else, they ended up fighting with each other. What idiots!

There were two guys holding Sid back and two more guys holding Rohit back. The funny thing was both Sid and Rohit didn't have the balls to hit each other.

'You loser fuck. Wasted your dad's money on LSE and still no job,' said Rohit.

'Whaat?? Look at you, you little pussy. Still a fucking techie. Get a life,' said Sid.'

Oh shit. No techie likes being called a techie. Ever.

'Who you calling a techie, you motherfucker?'

'Your dad.'

That was the cue. Both ran into each other and then started pushing and shoving and slowly but surely fell into the pool. And exactly like the scene from a few hours ago, first Sid was seen flying out of the house, then Rohit, then Mehtu and finally me. But before leaving, Sid looked at everyone and screamed.

'What the fuck are you all looking at? At least I didn't join my dad's business.'

We were about to leave when this smoking hot girl walked up to us and slapped Sid so hard, he almost fainted. She then threw a tissue at him, which he had given her.

It said: 'I want to be inside you. Love, Sid.'

Ouch. No wonder he got hit so hard. I put the tissue in my pocket and with that the grand night came to an end.

www.almamaterstore.in

We had to meet Mal's brother the next day for our website and I got busy doing some research on the web for our site. After I was done with my work, my mind wandered again to Facebook. I couldn't help but check out Arpita's profile and add her as a friend. What was a girl like that doing with that loser of a guy like Vinay. I did my usual check of Devika's profile but was completely startled with what I saw. Her profile pic had a guy with her in it. Oh Fuck! This can't be. Did she get a boyfriend? Her info page still said she was single. I clicked on the picture, desperately trying to find out who the guy was. And then I read the caption:

'My sweet bro and me in Ooty.'

Phew. Thank you Jesus for this.

I would have never been able to visit her profile again if it was actually her boyfriend. But the time of reckoning had finally come. The mouse went over the 'ADD AS FRIEND' button. This was it. I had to do it now. What was the worst thing that could happen? She would not accept my request? So? What's the big deal? There are a million fish in the sea. And besides, this is only the river, imagine the ones in the ocean. I can't be depressed if one fish rejects me. Okay, maybe I will get really depressed if she rejected me but I had to add her and get done with it. I was about to click and that's when the power went off. Divine intervention. Well, maybe I shouldn't add her. Not as yet.

Mal and I met at Shiva's again for a quick smoke before we headed out to his brother's office to meet him. As soon as we landed there, Shiva's boys took out their pens and pads. I was getting extremely suspicious about Shiva's plans and one of these days I was going to have to confront him.

While we got talking about the website, we realized we had a small problem at hand. You see, our company name was Alma Mater but the domain www.almamater.com was already booked. The next logical option was www.almamater.in but that was booked too. I guess we were definitely not the first ones to think of this name. So we had to choose from some other options.

www.almamater.co.in – Nah. People would get confused between .in and co.in

www.almamater.net – Nah. Everybody knows you should never get the .net. It's like being Buzz Aldrin while landing on the moon. You have to be Neil Armstrong, right?

www.almamater.org – What? We were not an organization. So we finally narrowed down our options to two domains: www.almamaterstore.in and www.almamatershop.com.

(Meanwhile, Shiva and his boys were scribbling furiously). Store sounded much better than shop and we decided to go with www.almamaterstore.in.

So that was it. Henceforth, we'd be www.almamaterstore.in.

If you're thinking of starting an internet company, go out there and check if the domain for the name that you thought of exists. There's no point coming up with a name but having no domain available for that. Funny as the name may sound, but you can check for domain availability at www.godaddy.com which is America's largest portal for domain registration.

Mal's brother's office was on Cunningham Road. As I have already mentioned, he ran a design firm called Exit Design. The company did branding, web design, product design etc. The best part was that it was Karn's company so we could expect a huge discount.

Both Mal and his brother are firm believers in numerology. So Rohan became Rohn and Karan became Karn.

His office was this really bohemian looking space on the top floor of the tallest building on Cunningham Road. All the walls were covered with movie posters and some crazy, whacky designs. There were no cubicles like the ones in Infotech and everyone seemed to have a Mac to work on. It was like an office out of *Dev D* or something. There were a lot of hotties working there too. Oh, I could so get used to this place. It looked really cool and he had an army of some really cool designers headed by this girl called Seema Seth. She was a graduate from Srishti School of Art, Design and Technology, which happens to be one of the best design schools in the country.

So anyway, we got talking with Karn about our company, our plans, our ideas and more importantly, our website, and why we wanted an e-commerce store. Karn was of great help to us because he gave us a questionnaire which would help us understand a few things about our branding.

Most young entrepreneurs jump into the waters without giving much thought to branding. When you're creating a brand you need to be very careful. You need to know why you are creating that brand, identify your target audience and the image that you are aiming to project. And Exit Design was going to help us with all of that, and much more.

Karn got all this information out from us. He was actually very impressed because we knew what we wanted.

'Most people who come here don't even know what they want,' he said. 'But I like you guys. At least you've got your head straight.'

This is extremely important if you're starting a company of your own. You should know the answers to all the 'WHYs'. Not only will it make things easier, it will also remove any ambiguity. For example, we knew we wanted to be an e-commerce store, we wanted to target the alumni and present students of schools and colleges, we knew that we wanted to be brash and young and we knew our core focus was going to be tees and hoodies. All of this would really help any designer to create your brand and website.

All this while, my phone was buzzing constantly. I was in this really important meeting and my mum was calling frantically. I knew what it would be about so I continued ignoring it. After a couple of hours we finally concluded the meeting. He assured us that he would help with our branding and build us a nice little website/e-store.

My phone was still buzzing incessantly. I looked at it. Twenty-seven missed calls and one message. 'Come home. ASAP. Mom.'

Yikes, what the hell happened now?

I ran to the nearest auto and imitated my mum.

'Koramangala,' I said.

'Two hundred rupees,' the auto driver said.

'Joking?'

I then proceeded to call the nearest policeman but guess what the cop told me? The loser told me to catch a bus if I couldn't afford the rate. I pleaded with him saying that the auto guy was overcharging, but he completely ignored me.

I went back to the auto and said, 'Okay, one hundred and fifty'.

'Sarry. No bargaining.'

How the fuck was I ever going to be an entrepreneur if I couldn't even negotiate with the auto guy?

So I had no choice but to go by that auto and pay the full fucking two hundred rupees. I finally reached my house in order to figure out what the problem was and the scene that greeted me was quite shocking.

There was mum sitting on one side of the sofa, tears rolling down her cheeks. There was Lalit sitting with his head on his knees. There was our maid, Sivamma, crying her heart out.

Oh man, this was bad.

Someone close to us must have definitely passed away or something. I felt really bad for not taking my mum's calls now. I walked up to her when Sivamma stopped me. She motioned to me that I wasn't supposed to go near her. I couldn't understand. What had happened? I went up to Lalit but he wouldn't say anything. I could almost hear the sad soundtrack of those old Hindi movies in the background. And then my mum looked at me.

'Varun,' she said, in the angriest tone I've ever heard.

'Yes mom.'

'Are you gay?'

Lightning. Thunder. Rain. And old Hindi movie soundtrack.

'Mom, what are you saying?' I said, looking suitably shocked.

'Answer me, Varun. Are you gay?'

I could not figure out what had made her think that way. Yeah I know I was spending way too much time with Mal, but gay? Seriously?

'No mom. Mother Swear.'

'Don't lie to me.'

'Why would you think something like this, mom?'

'Then what the hell is this?'

She threw a piece of paper at me. I just about managed to grab it.

'I want to be inside you. Love. Sid'

Oh shit.

'Oh mom, you should have asked me. This was given by Sid to a girl. She threw it back at us and I had kept it in my pocket. You should have asked me before jumping to a conclusion, no?'

'That's why I called you na, but you don't pick up the phone,' said my mother, dabbing her eyes with her pallu.

'Ha ha. Don't worry, mum. You have no reason to worry.'

'But you're sure, na?' She asked me again in a nervous tone.

'Of course, ma,' I said, giving her a hug.

On hearing this, Lalit and Sivamma ran out to celebrate in the rain. I was wondering if they would break into a Bollywood dance or something.

'But what do we do now?' my mum asked.

'Do what about what, ma?'

'I already told Anu Aunty.'

'Whaaaaaat?' I almost had a cardiac arrest.

'Pch, now I will have to go to her place and explain. These boys of today, na...' my mother tut-tutted.

And with that she left. But me, I was fucked. Now that Anu Aunty believed I was gay, the entire kitty party gang would believe the same. And their kids too, and their friends!

Okay. I was really fucked.

Down Memory Lane

While news about my sexual preference was spreading in Auntydom, word about our hoodies and tees was also spreading like wildfire. Cottonians had started calling us from everywhere asking us where they could buy our products from. Purshottam was going to take at least a month to finish up the order and therefore we couldn't take any new orders. But we knew that the idea had definitely hit. Now, we had to really get our website going and try and add as many schools to our list as possible.

In every city you have two rival schools or colleges just like Oxford and Cambridge, Harvard and Yale, Hindu and St. Stephens, and many more. In Bangalore, it's Bishop Cotton and St. Joseph's. The two have been the oldest and the best schools in this country for a long time and they have always had a love-hate relationship. The rivalry between the Cottonians and Josephites gets particularly intense during the Cottonian Shield which is an annual cricket tournament organized by Cotton and the matches are played the same fervour as an Indo-Pak cricket match. More often than not, the matches end in a fight.

Some of my really close friends are Josephites and when they came to know about the Cottonian stuff, they just had one question. 'Dude, where are the hoodies for the Josephites?' We knew, if we had done this for the Cottonians, we had to do this for the Josephites as well. Luckily for us, the Josephites were having their Old Boys' day a month later so it was perfect timing.

We repeated our ritual again and got some Josephite samples made. Then, as before, we met the principal of St. Joseph's and showed him the samples and told him about the company. With his blessings and with permission from the OBA (St. Joseph's Old Boys' Association) we were now ready for our second event in less than a month. This time around we pre-ordered the ready hoodies and tees from our manufacturer, Purshottam, to the tune of five hundred pieces each.

He was getting more impressed with us by the day. Not only had we lived up to our promise and placed a huge order for Bishop Cotton, we were now ready with the second school too. In fact, he was so happy that he agreed to give us a credit line. This meant we could now take forty-five days to pay him, which was a lot, and that really helped us later on. We were expanding. Slowly, yet surely.

My mum was still completely unaware of what was going on. Had she found out at that time, that would have been the last we heard of Alma Mater. I was still due to see the counsellor very soon and Anu Aunty was still scheming with

Biju Uncle to get me a job. Mom kept dumping more work on me. But the toughest job was that of cleaning up my room. There are two things you should never do—ask a girl her age and ask a guy to clean his room. However, I was left with little choice because if I didn't do this, then I would have to buy frickin' groceries.

Now cleaning a room that hasn't been touched for years was a monumental task. I couldn't even figure out where to start. I opened my old dusty cupboard and empty packets of Phantom cigarettes fell out. The strangest thing was that my long-forgotten cupboard kept yielding one memory after another. I ran into a lot of my stuff from school that had got lost in the decade gone by. I started thinking of all those wonderful days. And that is when it hit me. That is what Alma Mater was about! It was about bringing those good ol' days back. It was about taking you down that memory lane that leads to the wonderful times of school and college.

I still remember how Y2K was all the rage then. Only a handful of us had computers, yet everyone was worried how the virus would affect the machines. Nostradamus had apparently predicted that the world would end; but thankfully neither did Y2K cause a stir nor was Nostradamus right. (Thank god for that).

We didn't have Facebook then but we did have ICQ. One line none of us from that 'era' can ever forget is 'ASL (age/sex/location) please,' when meeting someone new on ICQ. We had atrociously funny-sounding email ids— therockrulez@hotmail.com, dude_am@indya.com and the like and even funnier names in the 'chat rooms'. You couldn't

Google but had to go to altavista.com or approach Mr Jeeves for any queries and clarifications.

You still had to call a girl on her landline and muster all the courage to ask for her. The only place you could hang out at was Wimpy's or McD and one still stayed away from the solitary Coffee Day on Brigade Road. Galaxy was where all the movies played and one had to stand in a long queue to buy tickets for *Mission Impossible 2*.

TV still played *The Wonder Years* and *The Crystal Maze* and the world seemed far smarter minus the Saas-Bahu soaps and the reality shows.

You could still find the time to read a book in the evenings and play cricket in your 'gully' on Sundays. 'Canada Dry' was the only source to get high and sweet, candy cigarettes were puffed at most of the times.

VSNL ensured porn still loaded one byte at a time and VCDs were all the rage. Hulk Hogan was perpetually rank one on all the 'Trump Cards' and Cameron Diaz from *The Mask* was in every puberty-hitting youngsters' dreams. The only operating system we knew of was Windows 98.

Anyone with a printer was treated with respect and the World Book Encyclopedia was the only source of information for projects. Hero Pen with the original Chinese nib was still preferred over the brash new 'Pilot' pen.

Azharuddin was still our captain and Jadeja and Robin Singh were our pinch hitters. Venkatesh Prasad was the only one with the balls to mess with the Pakis and we still lost all the test matches.

And I definitely cannot miss out wearing a 'colour' dress to school on your birthday and distributing Eclairs to everyone.

I could go on and on. But I guess you get the drift.

As I cleaned my room, I ran into my long forgotten collection of Tinkle. Gosh, how I used to love those comics.

I distinctively remember the first time I was ever caught by a teacher in class. She caught me because I wasn't looking at the blackboard. I was looking down. This was in the first standard. I was caught because I was reading a Tinkle.

I guess some of us might hate to admit it now but every one of us have read a Tinkle at some point or the other in our childhood. Even though it would be really un-cool to talk about 'Suppandi' now, he was the coolest character we knew in junior school. Before there was cartoon network, before Swat Cats took over, there was Uncle Scrooge on Doordarshan and there was Tinkle.

I remember how summer holidays would be the time when mum would pack us all in a train and take us to visit granny far, far away. The best part would be the train journey where one would spend hours reading Tinkle and waiting excitedly for the next big station to buy the latest series of the same. You'd be lost in the magical world of Suppandi, Kalia the Crow, Shikari Shambu and Tantri the Mantri.

I guess Tinkle comics have long been forgotten but they will always remain with us in our memories and will always remind us of times when things were simpler, when Bangalore was greener, when one would get up at 7a.m. on Sundays to catch Talespin on DD, when Phantom cigarettes ruled and chakra was more than just wheels. When we wouldn't worry about deadlines, meetings, Facebook and everything else that our lives have become today. We would only worry about when the next Tinkle comic would be out. Sadly, Uncle Pai, the creator of the series passed away recently. RIP Uncle Pai and thanks for the memories. We owe you way more than one.

So you see, Alma Mater was not just about starting another company. It was about starting a whole new sub-culture. Of making you feel like you were in school or college again—that wonderfully delicious feeling.

Gujju Boy!

I was still in the process of cleaning my room when I started getting frantic calls from Gujju Boy. This was quite strange for two reasons. For one, it was like 1 a.m. and Gujju Boy was usually never up so late and second, his parents are so strict that it wasn't possible for him to make a call at this time. I remember how, even after the tenth standard board exams, his mum used to force him to study for the IIT entrance exam. So there was no way he could make a call at this point of time evading his parents' scrutiny.

'Bob, can I crash at your place tonight?' said Gujju Boy.

'Why dude, what happened?' I said.

'Nothing dude, please tell me if I can come.'

'Sure man, but what happened?'

There was no response.

'Dude...'

And that's when he started crying. I mean I was no stranger to Gujju Boy crying. Once in school, when he got

21 out of 50 in Chemistry, he cried so hard he had to be sent back home.

I was getting worried. 'Bro, please tell me what happened...?'

'Dude...' he said, still sobbing.

'Tell me man, it's okay.'

I feared the worst.

'Uhm, dude, my mom caught me watching porn,' he said, crying.

I almost died on the spot.

'What?' I couldn't come to terms with this news flash.

Okay, this WAS shocking. You see, Gujju Boy is not the kind of guy who'd watch porn. In fact, he didn't care about porn at all. The only thing he cared about was getting into IISC or MIT or something. And what was worse was that I was finding this entire episode extremely hilarious, even though our dear Gujju Boy could not stop crying.

'Dude, that Sid gave me a porn CD. He told me to watch and be amazed,' he said, still crying.

'But why did you listen to Sid?'

'So I put it on when my parents were asleep. My mom woke up for water and she caught me,' he started crying even harder.

'Shit! Then?' I asked.

'She woke my dad up and they were very upset, they asked me to leave the house.'

'Oh shit...'

'Yeah dude, my life is over. Please let me in, please,' Gujju Boy broke down again.

Good lord! I hope my mom doesn't have to adopt him or something.

'Dude, don't worry, you come to my house,' I said.

In the next five minutes, there was a knock. It was Gujju Boy and he was still crying. After consoling him for like two hours, he finally went to sleep. Hopefully his parents will take him back someday. Hopefully.

Actually, I was hoping his parents would take him back the very next day—purely for his snoring.

Luckily for me, his parents did take him back the next day. I'm pretty sure he'll never be able to have sex for the rest of his life without looking over his shoulder.

Precursor to the Big Fight

A few days had passed and Mal and I were due to meet Karn and his team at Exit Design again. We landed there just in time and were happy to see that they had come up with the first drafts of our branding. They had given us four logo and colour options, they had even created a basic design template for our website and apparently this was not even the beginning. They said they still had to design tags, choose the right kind of paper, have more tees designed, design the inner labels; but all of that could only happen once the logo was locked.

We were, if that is possible, in a state of a jubilant shock; I mean we were at Noon Wines four months back getting smashed out of our brains and here we were choosing the logo for our company. The entire process was so exciting and besides, the logos they gave us were exactly the kind we were looking for. All in all, Exit Design gave us four options for our logos.

I really liked option 1 and 3 whereas Mal liked 2 and 4. That's where the problems started. For the first time ever we were having some differences. That was actually a very good thing because if both of us thought exactly the same way then there wouldn't be any point in being in business together, right? But the problem was that both of us had really strong personalities and each one of us was trying to dump their personal preference on the other.

'Okay dude, let's go with option 3. It's kickass, man,' Mal said.

'Dude, let's go with 1, man. It's simple, neat and uncluttered,' I said claiming all creative rights.

'Yeah and so is 3.'

Tempers were rising and a quarrel was imminent.

'Dude, what the hell do you know about design?' I said.

'What the hell do I know about design?? What the hell do you know?'

'Let's just go with fucking option 1.'

'No fuckface, we are going with 3.'

'Oh, so now I'm a fuckface, you dick.'

You know, when two boys get into business together they are bound to fight. We can't help it. We are wired that way. We're not like girls, we will fight it out right there and won't go bitch about each other to our friends. And besides, when two boys see way too much of each other there are bound to be some fights happening. Look at Steve Woz and Steve Jobs. They were at each other's throats in the first year at Apple. And Bill Gates and Paul Allen? We all know what happened there.

Just when this was going completely out of hand, Seema, Exit Design's lead designer stepped in.

'Guys, stop fighting. None of us like 1 or 3. We recommend option 2. And that is it,' she said.

Woah.

Now ideally, both Mal and I were not very happy with option 2 but it helped calm our egos. Our very overblown egos. So well, for the sake of egos, option 2 it was.

'Umm Seema, are you sure?' Mal sounded like he was Andy Warhol or something.

'Yes Rohn, option 2 works best,' Seema said.

'But Seema, you see…' I tried to stick my opinion in.

'Shut up, Varun. Option 2 it is,' she said.

Never ever try and design all this stuff for your own company even if your parents think you're very good at 'ART'. Leave it to the professionals. They will do a much better job.

Now that the logo was finally chosen, Exit Design went to work on creating the rest of our collaterals. This included a long list of things that we had never even thought of.

1. Website
2. Business Cards
3. Letterheads
4. Tags
5. Labels
6. Brochures
7. E-mailers
8. Tee and Hoodie Designs
9. Stickers
10. Brand Identity

I am glad we didn't try to do all of it ourself. Considering how badly we had fought over the logo, I can very well imagine what was going to happen if we tried working on these ten things listed above.

However, that minor logo incident had already created a small rift between us. Even Shiva and his boys had noticed the difference. The major blow came when I asked Shiva for an Ultra Mild while Mal smoked a Mild. We always smoked the same brand. There were rumours among the boys of a fight. We hadn't fought though. Not yet.

Meanwhile, Anu Aunty and my mum were getting extremely suspicious. I couldn't blame them. I was spending half my time at Shiva's and the other half at Exit Design, I had tissues in my pocket saying, 'I want to be inside you, Love, Sid', I had bunked two sessions with the counsellor and had already been accused of being gay. These aunties are quite smart and after all, they gave birth to you, so they will always be one step ahead. At all times.

I knew if my involvement in this business of mine was discovered, I would be shut down immediately. So I decided to go for one of the interviews just to be on the safe side. I was going to fail anyway, which was quite imminent, and that would calm them down for some time and at least give me some buffer.

When I told my mum I would go for the job interview the next day, she ran into the puja room to pray. I guess she had been praying a lot for this day to come. She then made a bunch of calls to her kitty party gang, informing them of what had just happened and then finally the call was made to Anu Aunty.

'Anoooo, guess what ya, Varun is ready for the interview.'

'Hawww, kaise?'

'I don't know ya. I've been praying to Babaji since morning, thanking him.'

'It has to be all your prayers to Babaji, ya Poo. You're such a strong lady, I'm so proud of you.'

And with that, both the ladies started the ritualistic sobbing. We should actually come up with a name for this culture of crying which I have always found very fascinating. It is the one stop solution for any occasion, good or bad.

Now, I was an average engineer at best. I mean I didn't even have an FCD (First Class with Distinction). I had just managed to scrape through with an average 60 per cent. I remember when my results came out, my parents shut themselves up for one full week, venturing out only to buy necessities. So, succeeding at the interview and getting the job was out of the question. 60 per cent is not good enough. Especially if you want to be a techie.

In Bangalore, they say, if you throw a stone randomly, you're most likely to hit a techie or a techie's manager.

So it was very surprising that Anu Aunty had set up an interview using all her pull with InfoTech—a techie company.

Pull is another typical Bangalore word. It denotes how much power or connection you have. For example, if you get into a fight, you call your 'pull'. Other cities have laid claims to have invented this but I'm certain this word was invented in the gullies of Bangalore.

I was still trying to figure out why Anu Aunty wanted me to get this job though. There was definitely some devious ploy behind all of this.

InfoTech was like any other tech company in Bangalore. A solid 9 to 5, Friday outings to a nearby resort for some team-building exercises, chances of going abroad if you're a topper and the works. I mean any techie would ejaculate just at the thought of working for InfoTech. My interview had been scheduled for Monday morning at nine which meant I had to get up at seven in the morning. The last time I woke up at seven was when I was in college, so there was only one way I was going to make it for the interview. I didn't sleep. I got ready by eight and was waiting for breakfast.

The house was strangely silent and I was wondering if I was ever going to get any breakfast. Mum suddenly emerged from the puja room with her usual entourage of Sivamma and Lalit. She had a big puja thali in her hands and started performing my aarti. A million prayers later she put a tika on my forehead and on those of her minions too, in case they felt left out.

She then looked at me and launched the token tear which got Sivamma and Lalit highly emotional. Before the Shashi Kapoor in me could come out, I ran away from there to the nearest auto stand. It was already 8.30 a.m. and I was too fucking late.

'Indira Nagar,' I told the auto driver.

'Two hundred and ten rupees,' he said.

'No chance. One hundred and fifty rupees,' and I gave him the 'I'm-gonna-call-the-traffic-police' look.

He didn't give a damn.

'Okay fine, two hundred rupees.'

What could I do? I was in a hurry.

I finally landed at the Tech Park where InfoTech was located. For some strange reason the security at these places is stronger than even the FBI offices. I had to sign and show my driver's license at three different checkpoints. The security guards seemed to think of themselves as CIA agents or something. I guess this kind of security made the techies feel really important about themselves.

I reached InfoTech and found a familiar and irritating face. It was the sissy Arjun who worked as a senior software developer there. He saw me in the hallway and I tried to act like I had not seen him. But he caught me and in his distinct, sissy voice called out to me, 'Varroon, hiii!'

'Arjun, wassup man?'

'So are you ready for the interview?'

Imagine a really effeminate voice saying this.

'Yup.'

'All the best, Varoon.'

I wanted to strangle the bastard.

My appointment was with Mr Ramaswamy who was the vice president of something. This was not the usual interview, you see, because Anu Aunty had used her 'pull', and therefore, I was directly meeting the top honchos.

'Ah, Varun, come, come. Anu has been telling me a lot about you.' Mr Ramaswamy said.

I shook his hands and sat down.

'So, have you brought your CV?'

I handed it over to him.

'Aha! Extra-curricular activities, very good. Debate, quiz, music, short films too. Impressive! Oh what's this? Only 61 per cent? Didn't study, ah?'

'Uh sir, I wasn't very interested in engineering.'

'Okay, okay, no problem.'

'Now, what's this? You got a KT (Keeping Terms) in fifth semester?'

'Sir, I didn't like engineering.'

'Okay, okay, no problem.'

'And what's this? Failed in lab in third semester?'

'Sir. I didn't like...'

'Okay, okay, no problem.'

'Arre, very poor marks in final year project.'

'Sir...'

'Okay, okay, no problem. Thank you Varun, we will call you.'

'Is that it, sir?'

'Yes, you can leave.'

Okay, this was really awesome. I mean I had prepared a bunch of rude answers to really piss them off but I guess my mediocrity must have completely shocked them. I mean why would InfoTech, of all places, hire a failure like me?

The Big Fight and a Lousy Offer

It was now August of 2009 and the first set of design options for all our collaterals was done. Karn had called Mal and me to come over and check them out. This was going to be really tough. I mean Mal and I hadn't spoken to each other properly after the day we fought. We didn't even go to Exit Design together that day and reached separately for the first time ever.

'Alright guys, so we have the first set of designs for you. Remember, no fighting,' Karn said.

Seema began to run us through our website and the rest of it. It was magical. I mean the way the site had been designed, the layout, the back-end—it was simply awesome. Mal shared my views and we were finally agreeing on things.

Now, let us get a little 'technical' here. An e-commerce store is built on platforms like Magento or OS Commerce. These are free and very easily available online. The kind of designs you can create on these templates is mind-blowing. The credit card payment gateway is provided by vendors like CC

Avenue. They give you a code and you simply have to install it and Voila! You have an e-commerce store. They charge about 3 per cent for every transaction which is not a big deal at all. So think of this, had we started a retail store, it would have easily put us back by ₹10-12 lakh and plus it had its drawbacks. You know how much the e-commerce store cost us? Only ₹2 lakh!

Seema went ahead and showed us the other collaterals. We loved the business cards and the letterheads. For a young entrepreneur, the pleasure of seeing his own, professionally designed business cards and letterheads is even better than sex. Trust me, it's multi-orgasmic. Things were going really well, even Exit Design was overjoyed, because for once, we didn't fight and seemed to agree in our preferences.

But our happiness was short-lived because soon we came upon the subject of tags and brochures. Mal wanted something and I wanted something else. We started shouting and screaming again. Even Seema couldn't intervene this time. We were almost going to take a swing at each other and had Karn not stepped in, things would have gotten really out of hand. I mean Mal is double my size, so the one ending up in a hospital would have been me.

As is customary, we stopped talking to each other. In fact, I landed up at Shiva's alone and his boys couldn't believe it. A big roadblock had entered our life, and that too at a very wrong time, because the first shipment from our manufacturer was due in a week's time.

I reached home in a fit of rage and saw my mum deeply engrossed in a puja again along with her entourage. The moment the saw me, Lalit ran to get some sweets and she ran towards me with a puja thali. She then proceeded to put a tika again on my forehead.

'Varun, god has heard our prayers. You've got a job,' she said.

Lightning, thunder and more lightning. Old hindi movie soundtrack and rain.

'What? Ma, what are you saying?'

'Yes Varun, your Anu Aunty has helped you get a job.'

'But they didn't even interview me.'

'I know beta. It was only a formality. Here's the letter.'

I glanced at the offer letter. Oh fuck. This was not for any technical position. This was a support job. I was going to be a call centre guy. I had to stay awake all night so that some dumb American who doesn't know what is wrong with his operating system can be at peace. No wonder Anu Aunty was so desperate to get me this job, so that I could be under Arjun for the rest of my life. This was the worst thing ever.

Ladies' Night

My life was really fucked up at this point. I had fought with Mal, I was supposed to join a call centre soon and I hadn't made any progress with Devika. In short, I was screwed. I needed a drink, or a smoke or a joint maybe? Frickin' anything.

I decided to meet Sid at Cirrus that night. We called Gujju Boy and Rohit, but Gujju Boy had been accepted back into his house only recently, so he couldn't screw around. Rohit, on the other hand, was googling MBA colleges abroad and was busy with that. So we decided to go alone, which was a huge risk, considering it was Sid.

Cirrus is a 'happening' place in Bangalore. It is like a lounge where you could have a few drinks with friends and it also has a dance floor in case you felt like breaking a leg. Wednesday nights are Ladies' nights and usually you will find quite a few nineteen-year-old girls getting drunk out of their skull, which was completely fine by us.

Sid said he knew a few female friends of his were going to be there so at least there was something to look forward to.

I met Sid at the entrance of Cirrus.

'Macha? All set to go?' he asked.

'Yep,' I was in no mood for any conversation.

'Let's go get some chicks, ma friend,' he said in that annoying tone again.

We entered Cirrus and as usual it was very dimly lit. The dance floor is right at the entrance so we could see the girls going wild as soon as we got in. Sid and I parked ourselves near the bar because there was no way one was going to find a place to sit on a Wednesday night. We started off with some hard tequila shots. Though they went down like a bomb, I really needed them.

I usually bail out early so was already a little high.

'Where are the chicks, dude?' I enquired.

'They coming, they coming. Patience, my nigga.'

As high as I might have been but Sid was pretending to be African-American again and that had got us into a lot of trouble last time.

It had been almost half an hour since his appeal to my patience and no women had showed up. Meanwhile, we were four shots down and pretty high by now. Things were looking really gloomy when the women finally decided to show up. No. Wait. These were not women. These were young girls, like eighteen young. I pulled Sid to the side.

'Sid, you fucker, who are these girls?'

'Easy nigga, they my cousin's friends. They wanted to see this place.'

'Dude, your cousin is fucking eighteen.'

'So were you once, dawg. Now enjoy.'

I knew it from the beginning. Going alone with Sid was going to be a disaster. I was already fucked in life and now we had to babysit these girls. The music was now reaching its peak and most of the crowd was on the dance floor, including us. Sid and I were dancing together like two idiots when he pulled me aside.

'Bro, one of the girls thinks you're cute. Go dance with her.'

'Dude, what the hell is wrong with you? They are eighteen, for god's sake.'

'You frickin' loser, you will never get anyone like this.'

And he pushed me towards Aahana who launched into a smile with all her braces showing.

'Heyyyy!'

Okay, so here's another thing about Bangalore. You see, with the advent of the International School System here, more often than not, you're going to find kids with a heavy American accent even if they haven't as much as crossed the border of Karnataka. These kids belong to the United States of Bangalore.

'Hey!'

'OK, so I'm like Aahana,' she said, with a thick Americanised accent.

'I'm Varun, nice to meet you.'

'Nice to meet you too. So, what do you like do like?'

'Well...I'm an entrepreneur.'

God, it felt so good to say it. Though I wasn't one yet.

'Ohmigod? Like really like?'

'Yup. And what do you do?' I said, trying my best not to show my complete disinterest in her.

'Okay, so I like jurst grraduated from school like. And now I'm gonna go to like Milan and do my fashion courrse therre like.'

The number of rrrs she rolled could give George Bush a complex.

'That's cool,' I said, trying my best to stay away.

The next thing I knew she put my arms around her and pulled me towards her. I was high and tried to resist but she wouldn't let go. I knew this was very wrong and had to stop. That bastard Sid was going to ruin me. I turned to my left and saw Arpita of all people grinding with her boyfriend. I looked at her and smiled but she gave me the weirdest look back. Obviously, I had an eighteen-year-old in my arms but thankfully, all of this was going to end soon because of Bangalore's 11.30 p.m. deadline.

But relief came sooner than expected as the girls had to leave. We reached the parking lot and got the girls safely into the car. Thank god they had a driver. They were so drunk they could kill someone.

'Varrrun, ohmigod, I had such a nice time,' Aahana said before they left.

'Yup, me too.'

This was really awkward because it was one of those 'should I hug or shake hand?' moments.

'OK, so can I like have your BB pin like?' she asked.

What? What happened to the good old times when you asked for the phone number?

Not like I had any intentions of giving her my number.

Before I could say my phone had conked off, Sid launched into a dictation giving her my BB pin.

God, how I wish Devika was here in the party. Maybe she was.

We were really hungry but there was absolutely no place to sit and eat. By now I was actually cursing the 11.30 deadline. I mean there used to be this restaurant called Empire which was open all night and served up some yummy ghee rice and chicken kababs but the other hotels got too jealous of Empire and that was shut down too.

I had no other option but to go home. I raided the kitchen and had given up all hope until I found the saviour. The greatest snack ever made. The snack that reinvented the uh...uhm...okay fine! I'm talking about Maggi. When you get drunk, there's nothing better in the world than the good ol' 2-minute-Maggi noodles.

I logged onto Facebook and was flushed with notifications.

One friend request: Aahana Thapar

Notificatons:

Aahana Thapar tagged you in a photo.

Aahana Thapar commented on your photo.

Aahana Thapar tagged you in a photo.

Aahana Thapar tagged you in a photo.

Aahana Thapar tagged you in a photo.

Aahana Thapar tagged you in a photo.

Aahana Thapar commented on your photo.

You were tagged in the album—'Girls' night out at Cirrus'.

I was going to kill Sid.

The Old Man and the What?

I was feeling really low the next day. Mal and I still hadn't resolved our issues. I guess our overwhelming egos precluded any hope of reconciliation. I mean that guy and I went to school together and I still couldn't walk up to him and settle the matter. Suddenly I began to wonder if this was the right path for me. I mean we had a great business idea but this constant quarrelling could only get worse. I was wallowing in my self-loathing when mum informed me that we had to go to Kolkata the next day for a wedding. Like it always happens with us, she had told me about this long back and as always, it had completely slipped my mind. This was good, I thought. I needed a change of air and I hoped I would be able to think with a clearer mind in Kolkata.

Cal, as I preferred to call it, was just perfect. The old colonial city was just the change I was looking for. It was as though I had gone back in time. The beautiful old bungalows, breakfast at Flurys, biryani from Arsalan and rounding up the night with drinks at Shisha, my cousins made sure they took good care of me. Maroo cousins are always like that, actually. They always take very good care. The next day I set out to explore the city alone in a hand-pulled rickshaw. And the story the rickshaw puller narrated to me changed my life.

When I was in the sixth standard, my cousin asked me if I was interested in reading his English textbook. I was already oppressed by my own books and the last thing I wanted was another 'textbook'. Out of sheer curiosity I asked him what it was that he wanted me to read and he mumbled something…

'The old man and the what?' I asked. He chucked the book at me and I stared at it. *The Old Man and the Sea* by Ernest Hemingway. Why would anyone want to read this? I decided to give it a shot anyway. That book changed the way I thought forever.

The reason I'm talking about the book is because it links up with the story that Bijoy, the really interesting rickshaw puller I met in Cal, narrated to me. Bijoy is unlike any other rickshaw puller you will ever meet. He speaks impeccable English and never spits his paan on the road, making it a point to do so only into the nearest bin. While he and I were stuck in numerous Cal traffic jams, he told me his story.

His father had been a wealthy businessman in a small town in Bengal back in the days. Bijoy went to the local English school but pulled out in the eighth standard to help his father. In the early '60s he decided to start his own confectionery business and opened a bakery. He named it after his wife and called it 'The Malti Devi Café'. He loved his wife dearly and after she passed away the café was all he had. The place served the best cakes in town and was extremely popular.

However, the formation of Bangladesh in 1971 completely ruined Bijoy's life. Being a Hindu, he was expected to move into India but his hometown did not fall within the Indian territory. He fought numerous legal battles to save the café and eventually lost all his money. After he was deported, his café was taken over by locals and renamed 'The English Café'. He had hired a lawyer in his hometown to fight his case. Since he had lost all his money, he had decided to start pulling a rickshaw and would save money every day to send to the lawyer.

For thirty-one long years he had pulled the rickshaw with the enthusiasm of a young man so that he could save enough money to pay the lawyer. In 2005, the judgment was passed and as expected, he lost all rights to the bakery. However, his lawyer was able to convince the judge of one thing, something which Bijoy wanted desperately.

He struggled for all these years to win his café back. He didn't succeed. But he goes to sleep every night knowing that there is a café in his hometown that serves the best cakes in town and it is called 'The Malti Devi Café'.

Bijoy is the old man in my *The Old Man and the Sea*.

He had opened my eyes. I got the motivation I was searching for. Now I was more determined than ever to get this company going. We were back in Bangalore the next day and the first thing I did when I landed back in town was call Mal. That was really tough. But I had to do it.

'Mal…,' I said

'Yo,' he replied, hesitantly.
'What's happening?'
'Chilling.'
'Shiva's?'
Silence.
Silence.
Silence.
Finally, 'Hmmm. Cool. Come.'

Let's Get this Party Started

Seeing Mal and me together got Shiva and his gang really excited. They had been praying for this day to come for quite some time, I guess. What was better was that both Mal and I ordered a Mild each, much to their joy. His boys gave us our ciggies and chai with a smile that radiated so much light it could guide ships.

We sat down there sipping our tea, smoking our ciggies and watching the traffic go by when I finally decided to break the ice.

'Mal, you remember that time when we went for a debate to Bishop Cotton, Shimla?'

'Yeah…'

'You remember I was supposed to participate in one of the debates but had prepared absolutely nothing'

'Yes, you fuckface, you woke up at 9 a.m. and the debate was at 9.15.'

'Ha ha, and I pretended to be sick and did a fake puke in front of you.'

'How can I ever forget that? And I knew you were faking it, you dick.'

'But you know what the best thing about that was? You covered for me, man. You didn't have to go and take part in the debate instead of me but you did that, man. You saved my ass.'

'I'm still waiting for the treat for that, you little prick.'

'Ha ha, and that's never coming.'

'Fuckface.'

'Dude, I'm sorry for everything, man.'

'Ujju, you're saying sorry? Now that's a first.'

'C'mon man, let's forget all of that.'

'Yeah dude, I'm happy you actually called me.'

Shiva and his boys almost cried.

Mal and I sorted our differences right then and there. We knew we couldn't go on like that and the truth was that we had made this company happen together. We couldn't throw it away over some stupid personal differences. Like Ari Gold from *Entourage* famously said—'We hugged it out, bitches'.

Now that we were done fighting, we decided to get to work right away. Simply put, our website was getting designed and our Cottonian shipment was coming in the next day. We now had to find a logistics partner for two reasons:

a) We had to send out all those Cottonian orders to the respective buyers. And therefore, we had to get cheap courier rates because we hadn't charged them for that.

b) We had to find a courier company that would take care of all our deliveries once the e-commerce store was launched.

Not only did we have to find a good courier company, we also needed very good terms.

As expected, our shipment arrived in perfect condition. None of us could keep the goods in our houses so we decided to store it in Sid's PG. Even though this could be a big risk, considering Sid could very well get drunk and puke on all the stock, it's not like we had many options.

We now needed to find a good courier company as soon as possible. So we called up that one number which deals with only contacts again—JUSTDIAL

It is surprising how young entrepreneurs fail to milk Justdial for contacts. For every aspect of our business we've used Justdial. You need a courier company? Call Justdial. You need an Accountant? Call Justdial. You need a web designer? Call Justdial.

The beauty of Justdial is that it doesn't give you only one or two contacts. It gives you a whole bunch of them. So we had the contact details of six courier companies and we decided to meet them to see if they would want to work with us.

The first three companies simply ignored us. I couldn't blame them. I landed up for the meetings in track pants and Mal was wearing chappals. They pushed us aside thinking we were one of those young wannabe entrepreneurs who had great ideas but no guts to implement them. But we didn't lose heart. We still had three more on the list. The first was DTDC. Their office was located in the heart of Bangalore on Commercial Street. While choosing our courier/logistic partners, there were only two requirements we had kept in mind:

a) They should give us a good rate for their services.

b) They should offer Cash on Delivery.

It might not sound like a big deal now, since all e-commerce companies are offering this service at present, but it was revolutionary back in 2009. There were only a handful of e-com. sites offering it then and not many courier companies had the service. 'Cash on Delivery' basically meant that customers paid for the goods they bought on the internet only after they received it. The courier guys collected the money and the courier company would then send a cheque due to us every fifteen days.

This method of payment is an extremely important component for any e-commerce business because not every Indian likes to use his/her credit card on the internet even if it is perfectly safe.

We entered the DTDC office and were ushered into the manager's office.

'Ah, boys, tell me, what can I do for you?' The manager said with his bald head shining away to glory.

We told him about our company and what we wanted.

'Ah, Cash on Delivery, eh? What volumes can I expect?'

We told him around twenty–twenty-five deliveries a day to start with.

'Ah, too less, my boys. You see we need at least two hundred.'

'That will come, Sir, but you need to give us time.'

'Ah, boys, no one has time these days. I like your spirit but you're too young.'

'But, Sir...'

'Ah, boys, I have another meeting now.'

I could have stuffed my fist inside his mouth if he opened it again to say 'Ah.'

We crossed off DTDC. Next up was Salim and Suleiman Couriers. The name was quite shady and their office was in an even shadier place.

Salim and his brother (you guessed it right, Suleiman!) were the proprietors of the company. They didn't have much of an office so we sat outside to talk.

'I like your idea. We are very much interested.'

A glimmer of hope. Finally.

'So you have Cash on Delivery service?'

'We don't, Sirji, but for you will start.'

Okay, this was already getting shady.

'Sirji, we deal all day with cheques and money. It's no problem.'

'Are you sure?'

'What sure, Sirji? See...'

He then proceeded to open one of the parcels and displayed a cheque.

This was getting shadier by the minute. He opened a customer's package.

'Just you watch, Sirji, we will do great for you.'

'Okay, so where does the bulk of your business come from?'

'Overseas, Sirji.'

'Overseas?'

'Dubai, Sirji.'

My brain went on a screaming spree: GET OUT, GET OUT! And we gladly obeyed.

The last company on our list was Aramex. We were really excited about Aramex because we knew they offered Cash on Delivery and a few e-commerce sites that we had stumbled upon used Aramex as their courier partners.

Their office was located in Indira Nagar and we just about managed to get there in time for the meeting.

Luckily, the country head was in Bangalore at the time so we got to meet the top boss directly.

'Guys, I really like the idea. It's unique and hasn't been done before. But what's the bandwidth?'

'Sir, you could expect small numbers to start with, but as the brand and the company grows the numbers will be substantial,' Mal said, clearly creating a good impression.

'Hmm. But you guys still don't have your website and branding in place.'

'That's getting ready even as we speak. Should be done in a month's time.'

'So you will want Cash on Delivery also, I'm guessing.'

'Of course sir, that's very important.'

'Hmm. See, I'll give you the best rates for shipping. I can convince my bosses to get Aramex to partner with you guys. I really like your idea. I used to be like you all when I was young and wanted to start my own company once. But I can't promise Cash on Delivery as yet.'

'But sir… '

'You see guys, if we start getting decent volumes from you, then we will start Cash on Delivery in no time.'

'Sir, please think after putting yourself in our place. Imagine if you were young and you wanted to start this company and the whole world was against you. How would you feel? You know we got chucked out of the three other courier companies we went to. And do you know why? Because we were too young. Sir, please don't let our age be a limiting factor here. We really need Cash on Delivery because a lot of our customers will be students who don't have credit cards.'

He thought for a while. A whole ten minutes passed before he finally said, 'Okay, you can have Cash on Delivery but only on the launch of your website. Not before that.'

'Thank you, Sir. Thank you so much.'

Wow! We had done it. Finally. Though we couldn't get Cash on Delivery now which meant we would personally have to deliver all the Cottonian stuff ourselves, we did have a logistics partner in place. A wave of confidence swept inside us again. We got an auto to go home.

'Koramangala.'

'Two hundred rupees.'

'Hundred and no more.'

'Nah.'

'Okay, die!' and I began to walk away.

'Wokay. Come Saar.'

Aunties in Hot Pursuit

The date for joining InfoTech was coming near. Anu Aunty had, by now, reached cult status amongst her friends and people from far and wide were calling her to help their kids with jobs or counsel them or to help them get married. Anu aunties of India have been the driving force behind the fact that very few people in this country dare to think out of the box. Because the moment someone begins to think out of the box, the Anu aunties of our lives emerge from nowhere and stomp on our plans.

By now I had gotten really busy with Alma Mater. We had to sign off on the final designs, the development work for our website had to begin, the shipments to all the Cottonians had to be sent out, the Josephite orders were due soon, and there were a million other things to attend to.

All of this was getting my mum and Anu Aunty extremely suspicious. Rumours were abuzz in kitty party circles and everyone was wondering what Poornima's son Varun was up to. The ladies knew I was getting up at ten and running out of the house these days. They knew they could no longer count on me to run their errands or give my ignorant opinion on the latest sarees they bought. There was trouble brewing and the aunties hated it when they were not in tune with the latest gossip.

If this wasn't enough, I was getting spammed on my blackberry with jokes from Aahana Thapar. One would not have too much of a problem if the jokes were good, but they had such strong sexual undertones that they made me squirm.

Sample this:

Broccoli: I'm not happy with my looks. I look like a tree.

Walnut: You don't have any reason to complain. Look at me, I look like a brain.

Mushroom: Dude, I look like an umbrella.

Banana: Can we place change the topic? ☺☺☺☺

(Smileys??Are you kidding me??)

I was leaving for the day to Shiva's to discuss some important business matters with Mal but there was a big roadblock. Anu Aunty was there along with Neelu aunty and mum. I had to hold my nerve here. This could get very tricky. Indian aunties are the finest interrogators in the world and are capable of getting any information out from anyone.

'Oho! Varun, congrats dear, new job 'n all.'

'Thank you, Neelu aunty. All credit to Anu Aunty though.'

'So when are you treating us ya?' Anu Aunty demanded.

'Soon aunty, soon.'

'So where are you going now?' enquired Anu Aunty.

There you go.

'Oh, nowhere aunty, to the library. Reading up before I join my job.'

'Which library?'

'Aunty, uh, it's here only.'

'Oho, where only ya?'

FUCK

'Near 4th cross, aunty.'

'Neelu, which library is there near 4th cross?'

'Aunty, it's new, you wouldn't have seen it.'

'I don't know ya, something is fishy. Your mom tells me you're always out, what's going on?'

'Oh nothing, aunty.'

'Varooon, you can run but you can't hide.'

OH FUCK, FUCK.

'Chalo, anyways, carry on.'

The aunties by now were in hot pursuit. There was something that was going on and they didn't know about it and that pissed them off the most. I had to watch my back from now on. I had informed Shiva and his boys and they promised that even if they got bribed they weren't going to sneak on me. I left no tracks at home and all company papers, cards, letterheads etc. were now safely stored at Sid's. Okay, not safely, but they were there.

Business 101

As per our deal with Aramex we could only get Cash on Delivery on starting our website. This meant that we had to personally deliver the products till then and collect the money from the customers while making the deliveries. The problem was we were not talking about fifty or hundred packets. We were talking about five hundred and fifty. It was going to be a mammoth task. I mean, here we were the hotshot co-founders of a brand new company but what people didn't know was that we were also the gofers, office boys, delivery boys and everything else.

We started off by packing the goods in nice little Alma Mater courier packets. We had personalized the courier packets with our logo and website embossed on it.

Never forget this, guys. Place your brand name wherever you can. Anywhere.

The packing itself was a humongous task. Packing five hundred and fifty courier packets is no mean task and it took us two full days to complete this shit. When Sid wasn't drunk or stoned or watching porn he helped us out. But that was minimal. Very minimal.

Once we had all the packages ready, that was when the real hard work started. We decided to spread the deliveries over ten days. We would take fifty packets everyday and had to go all around Bangalore delivering them. We divided the packets based on the areas and luckily for us, Bangalore was not as big as Delhi or Bombay. But one thing was for sure—it was the most tiring job of my life. We would get up at 7 a.m. and start deliveries by 8. We would go on all day without lunch or any major break just trying our best to finish off the fifty packets. More than half of our time would be spent finding the houses and the worst part was, we could never stop to take rest because we had to meet our target of fifty or those shipments would get piled onto the next day.

However, indirectly this was actually of the greatest help to our newly formed company. For one, we would personally deliver these packets, so it instantly helped us network with a lot of our customers. You see, Cottonian alumni consists of a lot of CEOs, CFOs, managers, artists and other eminent personalities. So indirectly, we were building a future network base for our company. We would chat with them, exchange cards, exchange business ideas and more importantly, network. Something that would go on to help us immensely later on.

I think you guys already know this but if you're thinking of starting your own company, never forget one major thing—networking. You need to sell your company shamelessly. Like everywhere. During the initial days of Alma Mater, I practically lived in one of our Cottonian hoodies. Networking is the key, and if you want be an entrepreneur, forget about being shy.

Delivering these packets was one of the greatest learning experiences ever. Through this one exercise we learnt something very important. Starting a company is not about getting a flashy office and calling yourself CEO. It's much more than that. If you really want to start a company you should be dead passionate about it. Even if it means becoming courier boys for twelve full days from morning till evening! Phew.

I was still recovering from the ten days of back-breaking days of hard work. Making all those deliveries had gotten the best of me and I was trying to get some sleep but my phone was constantly buzzing.

It was Sid.

'Dude, why are you not picking up my call?'

'I want to sleep you shit, what is wrong with you?'

'Dude, come I got tickets, we're going for *Transformers*.'

'Dude, I wanna sleep. I'm not interested.'

'Aye come dude, I already bought the tickets.'

'Damn you!'

I got myself out of bed with much difficulty. I was in no mood to go for this thing but these guys were getting senti because I hadn't met them for a long time, so I had to go.

Forum Mall is one of the biggest malls in Bangalore. In fact, it's Bangalore's first ever mall. It holds a special importance in my life. This is where I had my first kiss in PVR cinemas. But I was going there now with three boys.

I reached there and found Sid all dressed up.

'What's wrong with you? Are you going for someone's wedding?'

'Okay dude, don't get pissed.'

'What happened?'

'Ah, nothing much.'

'Go on, tell me you fuck.'

'We didn't get tickets for *Transformers*.'

'What? You fool, you should have told me. I'm going home to sleep now.'

'But we got tickets for *P.S. I Love You*.'

'What? Dude, is something wrong with you? Four guys going for *P.S. I Love You*?'

'Ah dude, there's another problem.'

'Oh fuck no. They're not coming?'

'Eh, sorry dude.'

'Dude, I'm NOT watching *P.S. I Love You* with you.'

'Eh dude, another problem.'

And that's when they showed up. Aahana 'like' Thapar and her annoying friend. I was gonna kill Sid, better still, I was going to fucking chainsaw Sid.

He quickly pulled me aside.

'Dude, I'm this close to getting this girl, the only way she would come is if Aahana would come. And Aahana would only come if you...'

'Dude, are you fucking serious?'

'Dude, please man,' Sid pleaded with me.

Ah! What all people do for friends.

'Ohmigod, hiiii!' said Aahana and that was the most annoying tone I had ever heard.

'Oh, hey!'

'I didn't imagine like you would be like interested in chick flicks like…'

'Yeah, I see them sometimes.'

'Ohmigod, that's so cute!'

'Uh, yeah…'

And Aahana ran away to giggle with her friend. She mumbled something into her ear and they giggled even more after that. I have never been able to figure out why girls like to giggle so much.

The two hours I spent watching that movie were the longest two hours of my life. And watching Sid make out with that girl made it even worse. I kept taking a lot of bathroom breaks and just about managed to get through it. But the worst part was the camera again. Why do girls have to take pictures whenever they go to a club or a movie or for dinner or for sleepovers or fucking anything. There's a camera everywhere and all of it eventually shows up on Facebook. Also, all girls seem to have this trademark picture of their feet together or their shoes together. And no picture is complete without the infamous 'pout'. They must have snapped like fifty pictures of all of us together. I was already having nightmares and one thought bothered me more than anything else—the album name!

Legal Eagle

The next day Mal and I were at Shiva's as usual, discussing Alma Mater when both of us got a text from Seema. 'Guys, come to the office, it's urgent.' We landed at Exit Design two hours later and were completely surprised. It was our collaterals—cards, brochures, tags etc. all printed and done. I almost had an orgasm seeing them. WOW. I mean till now we had seen all of this on a computer screen but we were holding all of this shit for real now. I was feeling like a teenager in a porn video store. This was so awesome. We had imagined all of this but this looked way better than what we had visualized.

Now that all our collaterals were in place, our designs were ready and our website was a work in progress, it was time to take care of the legal stuff. The first and only person you need for these things, like getting your company registered etc., is an accountant. And like we did for everything before this, we called Justdial. We found this amazingly sweet accountant whom we called Dee uncle. Both Mal and I were partners, so in order to register this company we first needed a partnership agreement. But neither of us had seen an agreement before nor did we know what went into one. So we did what every twenty-first century kid would do. We googled. On googling 'partnership agreement templates' we found a host of options for us to choose from. We chose the simplest one and added two–three points we deemed necessary. We got these typed on a stamp paper, signed and sent them to Dee uncle along with a bunch of other requirements like copies of driver's license, passport photos, address proof etc.

Since we were a product company we needed a VAT certificate to make sales. It takes a token fee of fourteen thousand rupees to get the certificate. Once the company is registered as a partnership and you have a VAT certificate, you're ready to go. So from now on, every month we had to give 5 per cent of all our sales to the government.

All of this must have taken not more than two weeks. We got our PAN (Permanent Account Number) card eventually and Alma Mater was now legal. The time had now come to open our bank account and also settle some of our bills. We needed to pay our manufacturer for the first shipment he had sent. We also needed to pay Karn an advance for the design charges. The money we made from the Cottonian sale helped settle half the amount we owed Purshottam but we still needed more money.

I was never in the habit of saving but had around ninety thousand in my account which I had saved up from my odd filmmaking jobs over the past year. Mal, on the other hand, was working for KGMP and was thus eligible for a loan.

Mal took a loan of ₹1 lakh in his name and I busted out all my money and we put this into the newly formed bank account of Alma Mater. I had saved the money to buy a new camera. But I could buy my camera later, probably even ten cameras, if Alma Mater succeeded. My company needed money now and I had to give it everything I had.

It is moments like these when everything becomes real— when you have to put every penny you earned into something you believe in.

We were now a legal company with an official bank account. The time to inform my mum about this was coming close. I had to do it soon, if I didn't want to work for InfoTech, that is.

Kitty Party

The following day, preparations were in full swing at my house. A kitty party was being organized and this time it was my mum's turn to host it at our place. These parties are like the Cricket World Cup where every nation gets to host it once. This kitty party was coming back to our house after a long time.

My mum's minions were in full flow that day. They had made the house look like it had been built just yesterday. Mum did all the cooking, as was the ritual in all kitty parties. If even one of the aunties found out that the food had not been cooked by the lady of the house, it could lead to an immediate ouster from the gang and no aunty wanted that.

These parties are a great place to be for anyone with an appetite for gossip. Whose husband is earning more, whose kids are doing well and who bought the latest diamond earring etc.—you will get answers to all these and many more questions. Usually, the kitty parties are meant only for aunties but my mum and Anu Aunty specifically insisted that I stayed for this one. It didn't take an Einstein to find out why? They wanted to know what I was up to.

'Hiiii Neetuuuu!' Anu Aunty screamed as she hugged Neetu aunty as though they were long-lost sisters. Both of them hated each other. You see, Anu Aunty's husband was now working under Neetu aunty's husband, even though both started out at the same time in the same company.

'Arre Smita, nice earrings ya. Where you got?' Rupa aunty enquired. Smita aunty's husband was in the customs department and all the ladies suspected foul play.

'Ooo this paneer is just melting in my mouth ya Poo. Teach me also na…' Usha aunty said, praising Mom's culinary skills.

'He he. Arre the paneer is from Nilgiri's ya…'

The gossip continued and more aunties began to pour in. Sivamma was running around carrying sherbet for everyone, music from Karan Johar films was blaring from the music system, and there were all these aunties wearing fine sarees and expensive jewellery. The peace of my house evaporated suddenly and the innocent walls were forced to hear the darkest secrets of every aunty.

Some aunties noticed me, some didn't. I was a no-good, jobless loser so none of them saw me as a potential husband for any of their daughters in the future. So nobody actually cared.

'Arre, Varun beta, what are you doing here?' they said laughing their hearts out.

'What ya still no girlfriend, eh?' said another as she stuffed a gulab jamun in her mouth.

Yeah I know a lot of gay jokes were going to come my way.

'So when is the job starting, Varoon?'

Sitting idle, a funny comparison came to my mind—a kitty party somewhat resembled an engineering classroom. You see, an engineering classroom gets segregated into different gangs at the start of the very first semester. First, you have the CET rank holders. They are a species in their own right. They generally hang out amongst themselves, mugging day and night. They hold each other's hands wherever they go. There are usually very few or no girls in this group and they watch a lot of porn. Like a lot. Second, you have the studious girls. They usually dress in ethnic wear, never talk to boys, always have the best notes on any subject and hate the 'mean girls'.

Third, you have the local gangsta boys. They love everything local. Local movies, local songs, local food. They have big bikes and speak only in the local language. They watch a lot of porn too and the CET boys usually get their porn from these boys.

One obviously can't forget the 'mean girls'. These are the not-so-hot girls who suddenly become super-hot because there are hardly any girls in an engineering college. They hate everyone and everything. They come in their fancy cars and never mingle with the lesser beings of an engineering college.

And last but not the least, you have the ICSE/ISC boys. These are the boys who have been brought up in big public schools, they speak impeccable English and try and hit on the 'mean girls'. They watch a lot of porn too.

Similarly, you have a very distinct segregation in a kitty party. First you have all the cool aunties whose husbands are the top honchos of big companies. They form their own separate gang and deride everyone in sight. They consider the current kitty party too unworthy of their attention and are always on the look-out for a higher social circle.

Then there are the drama queens. Their sole aim in coming to these parties is to vent their frustration about their husbands, their children and shed a tear or two in the process. Along with them are the gossip girls. These are the aunties who are the life-blood of all kitty parties. They have information about anyone and anything. They are the walking-talking Google search engines for the kitty. And last but not the least, there is one ringleader. It's not a declared position but everyone respects that one aunty. That aunty in this case happened to be our very own Anu Aunty.

The problem was, I was messing with the wrong aunty. I mean you can mess with anyone else but not the ringleader. If you mess with Anu Aunty, you mess with the entire kitty party. Sooner or later, she was going to find out about Alma Mater and also the fact that I wasn't going to join InfoTech.

The kitty party usually reaches its crescendo with the game of housie. All the ladies sit around and Anu Aunty is given a special chair.

'Shall we start?'

'Anu, tell na?'

Anu Aunty then gives her blessings.

'Chalo, let's begin.'

Like a committee investigating a fraud case or something.

And with that they begin.

Even though I really hated kitty parties, it would actually go on to help me a lot with my marketing and branding later on.

It's my sincere advice to you guys, if you ever get a chance to sit in on of these kitty parties, don't pass.

Rohit Gets a Girlfriend

It was Rohit's birthday and the fatso was giving us a treat for like the first time in his life. Okay fine, maybe this was the second time, but the first treat was so pathetic it didn't count. He better did, I mean he had been a techie for a good one year and easily had a lot of money stashed up. He took us out to a pretty famous Bangalore joint called Spiga's.

Spiga's is an awesome restaurant in the heart of Bangalore. The food is excellent there and the blueberry cheese cake is the most awesome thing ever. Every Bangalorean has been to Spiga's at some point or the other.

Also, apparently Rohit had some big news for us. When it comes to Rohit, the big news can only be, 'Guys, I got into Carnegie Mellon,' or 'Guys, I got into Duke.'

The man was an MBA dictionary on two legs and his life revolved around two things—jerking off and GMAT.

Spiga's is a chick-magnet place. All the pretty women show up here usually on a Friday night. Rohit had chosen the right time and place for his treat which was quite surprising because the last time he ever treated us was at Shanti A/C Veg. Restaurant. This was certainly a step up. Like a big step up. He was already there when I reached and was gleaming as though he'd gotten into Harvard, but thankfully Rohit was not that smart. The boys trickled in one by one. There was Sid as usual, and Mehta the Gujju Boy. Rohit had also invited two of his work buddies, Venkatesh and Roshan. As expected it was a sausage fest and we were toasting to another boys' night out which must have now been like the millionth one. Rohit started the proceedings by ordering a chilled bottle of champagne—though the cheapest one on the menu.

Oh Fuck! Maybe he did get into Harvard.

'Boys, tonight we drink like bitches.' He screamed, obviously audible to the elderly lady near us who gave me a dirty look because of this fool.

'What's the big news, da?' Sid asked impatiently.

'Patience, machan. Patience,' I said.

We were surprised by the spread the waiter started bringing in. Thai curry with rice, some Asian steak, penne with vodka, some wonderfully soft pizzas along with an unlimited supply of booze. We were getting hammered again. Literally.

'Psst, Varun, guess what? Sid whispered to me.

'Tell bro.'

'You know that girl Shivani?'

'Who is Shivani?'

'The one with the insanely cute ass, dude.'

'Who, da?'

'Aye fucker, the one Rohit liked.'

'Oh yeah, what about her?'

'Bro, I made out with her yesterday.'

'Whaaat? Get out of here!'

'No bro, really.'

'How the fuck?'

'Dude, we were all at Opus last week. She was hammered and needed a drop home.'

'You fuck, you couldn't have.'

'Dude, it's not like I took advantage of her, she was really turned on.'

'I can't believe you. You know Rohit likes her like crazy.'

'He he, dude, all of us like girls, it's not like Rohit is gonna get her or something.'

The booze kept flowing and as expected our spirits were very high again. Venkat and Roshan who seldom drank were now boisterously high.

'You know rascals, I got rank fifty-four in the CET. Even your dad could not have managed that,' said Venkat.

'Ha ha, he is furny, aye,' commented Roshan.

Our Roshan was a Mallu boy.

'I gort rarnk thirrrrteey four.'

A war of the techies was about to begin when, luckily, Sid interrupted.

'Aye guys, dump the ranks. Rohit, what news you got for us, dude?'

'Soon boys, soon. Let the clock strike twelve,' said Rohit.

Meanwhile Sid pulled me to the side again.

'Dude, that was the best fucking night, dude.'

'Ahm, okay...'

'What an ass...'

I was least interested in hearing about his sex life.

Sid continued with descriptions of his exploits and Venkat and Roshan couldn't shut their trap about CET. To make matter worse, I was still being bombarded with Aahana's jokes on my Blackberry while we were at dinner.

'Okay guys, round up.' Rohit finally said. Phew.

This night was finally going to come to an end.

'Okay guys, here's the thing. I got lucky twice today. I got a hike in my salary (Venkat and Roshan started clapping) and I asked someone out.

Wait. What? No, are you serious? Rohit got a girl and I didn't?? NO, NO, NO.

'Oooh. Nice da, Rohit. Who's the girl, da?' Venkat and Roshan obviously couldn't believe this could be happening too.

You know they are right when they say that you actually don't feel that great when your friend does well.

'She is coming boys, she is coming. Oh wait, there she is.'

We saw her walking towards us. Rohit had scored big time. We couldn't see her face yet, but she did have a cute butt.

'Cute ass!' all the boys present around the table said in unison.

And then she turned around. She was Shivani!!

Apple is More than a Fruit

I had developed a good reading habit during the past one year and had got addicted to a lot of biographies of crazy entrepreneurs. These books are of great help because you get to peek into the lives of all these amazing people and the things they've gone through.

One person's life influenced the way I think and my life substantially. It was Steve Jobs, the founder of Apple Inc. who passed away recently on 5 October 2011. His story is one of the greatest comeback stories in history.

Steve Jobs and Steve Wozniak were friends who together started Apple back in the '70s. Wozniak was the inventor and he invented the Apple computer and Jobs went out to sell it and got the company going. Apple, even in those times, was the pioneer of design and technology. The company did wonderfully well in the initial years and its IPO (Initial Public Offering) was the biggest ever in American history after Ford Motor Company. Steve Jobs was a millionaire many times over even in his twenties and the head of one of the coolest computer companies in the world.

But then, things began to go wrong. Steve Jobs apparently started creating an internal conflict among the employees of Apple. The board was not too happy with him and they decided to remove him from the company. Imagine, the guy started Apple, sustained it through all those initial hard years, put his life into the company and six years later, just like that, they threw him out!

Not one to give up, he went on to start another company called NeXT, paving way for some of the most cutting edge technology of its time. He also launched a computer animation company along with NeXT.

The '90s turned Steve Jobs' life around and got him what he deserved. Apple, which had faded away and was now in the dumps, badly needed a new operating system software. Thus, they decided to buy NeXT.

So here's the deal, this guy gets chucked out of his first company, starts a new one and a few years later sells this company to the first company he originally founded. And you know how much he sold NeXT to Apple for? Five hundred million dollars! That automatically brought Steve Jobs back into the board of Apple and a few years later he became the CEO and the rest, as you all know, is history.

Oh! and that animation company he founded—that was Pixar—one of the most profitable animation companies in the world. He sold that to Disney for seven fucking billion dollars and became the single largest shareholder of Walt Disney Co.

What would you and I have done if we got chucked out of our own company? We would have killed ourselves. This guy, however, not only takes back Apple but in a few years, turns it into one of the biggest companies in the world, worth almost three hundred billion dollars. I don't even know how many zeroes come in that!

Oh F**k and the Big Confession

It was September of 2009 now and the Josephite Old Boys' Day was in a day's time. We had a huge shipment coming in again consisting of all the Josephite tees and hoodies. Sid was now getting really irritated with all the boxes and we had to find a new place for them soon. We had already placed another big order for the other schools and colleges whom we had received permission from and the only thing preventing the world from getting to know about us was the website which was going to get done very soon. Or at least we hoped so.

The next day we took all the cartons, all twenty-five of them, in two separate cars to St Joseph's. Old Boy's reunions were something we had become experts in. We had set up our stalls in no time and had all the necessary stuff displayed. This time around, we actually had a handsome stock of tees and hoodies to sell. There would be no taking orders and doing home deliveries by ourselves.

Unlike Bishop Cotton, the boys started coming in as soon as we started the stall and thankfully they really liked our stuff. The sales were brisk and again we got to meet the top honchos of many companies. Our brand name was slowly spreading and some even commented they had heard about us from their Cottonian friends. The word of our quality was spreading and that was doing a lot of good for us in terms of marketing.

You know what guys, before you start a company, get the basics right. Spend a lot of time and money on quality. If that's taken care of, people will automatically tell their friends about it and you will not have to end up spending lakhs on marketing. There's nothing better than word of mouth when it comes to spreading the word. Trust me.

Mal had just stepped out for a break and I was handling the stall alone. There was such a rush, I didn't even have the time to see anyone. Suddenly a familiar voice asked me something.

'Hi, how much for the hoodie?' The voice was peculiarly effeminate.

'Five hundred bucks, dude,' I said, without even looking up.

'That's expensive, Varun.'

Woah. WTF?

I looked up and it was Arjun. Arjun with that effeminate voice and style of his. What the fuck was he doing here? He was not even a Josephite.

'Arjun, uh, what are you doing here?'

'Oh, our family friend Rahul is here ya. We came with him.'

'Ah, okay… How's Anu Aunty doing?'

'She's fine ya, she's here, wanna meet her?'
OKAY, I'M SCREWED.
'Ahem, no man. Chill, what's the hurry?'
'But dude ya, is this a hobby or something?'
'Uhm, kinda man.'
'Well you better shut it down soon ya. You starting at Info on Monday, no?'
'Uh, yeah, well actually...'

Before I could say anything that dumb fuck called out to his mum, 'Mummy, mummy, here,' and started waving like a little girl.

And that's when she entered. My pulse was running high, I had literally frozen. My game was up.

'Haw, Varun, what are you doing here?'
'Uh aunty...'
'Arre, and what's all this? Does Poo know?'
'Uh...'
'Chee, are you a T-shirt salesman now?'
'Uh, no aunty... '
'Baap re. This is shocking ya. Is this what you been up to?'

Everyone around us had stopped talking. They were all looking at us. It was as though I had smuggled these tees in from Dubai and Anu Aunty had just busted our illegal operation.

And that's when Mal walked in coolly.

'Hain? Rohn, even you?' she asked Rohn, surprised.
Like Mal had helped me murder someone.

'Oh yes, Aunty. Varun and I are in business together, don't you know?'

Mal pulled me aside and said, 'I had to do this, you ass. You didn't have the balls, so someone had to let it all out.'

Gulp.

As expected, I got a call two minutes later. It was Lalit.

'Bhaiya, come. Mummy ji crying.'

I was done.

Sid filled in for me and I rushed home to take care of the 'situation'.

As I rushed to an auto, I saw a big poster on the wall which said—'Above Mother There is No Other'.

The scene at home couldn't get worse. Mum was leaning her head sideways on the sofa. Tears were rolling down her cheeks. Her minions were no better. Lalit was crying too and Sivamma was behaving as if someone had passed away. The scene was extremely gloomy and this time I had no one to help me. There was no Mal, no Sid, no Rohit, no one. I had to deal with this alone and tell her once and for all.

'Mom', I said and she started crying even harder.

The moment my mum increased the volume of her sobbing, her minions followed suit making it tougher for me.

'You lied to me, you lied to me,' she cried.

'Mom, no, I didn't.'

'You let me down. You're no longer my son.'

THUNDER, LIGHTNING, RAIN. OLD HINDI MOVIE SOUNDTRACK.

'Ma, you're being overdramatic.'

'Go away, Varun, I don't want to talk to you.'

'But mom, 'and she started crying harder.

And so did her minions.

'Okay ma, I'm going to tell you a story. After listening to this story you do what you want, okay?'

No response.

'Remember on our flight back from Kolkata I was talking constantly to a man next to our seat?

His name was Mr Rajan. Mr Rajan is who you want me to be. He is Harvard educated, doctorate from Kellogg, worked for all top-notch firms and is currently a VP at one of the big four. The fact that he was traveling 'cattle class' with us itself was surprising. I was going through some of my Alma Mater letters and Mr Rajan chanced upon one of our brochures. He saw them and was very pleased with the idea and thus we got talking on a myriad topics ranging from investments, VCs, funding, scaling up etc.

He then told me about his friend Ashok. Ashok and Mr Rajan went to IIT Bombay and graduated in 1971. Ashok stood at the top of the class, gold medalist, scholarship and all that. He was voted by his peers to be the one who was most likely to make his first million by the age of thirty.

Ashok and Mr Rajan both got accepted into Harvard's prestigious business programme. 'Ashok had an immense fascination for cars,' Mr Rajan told me. Both worked really hard but it was tough for most students to match up to Ashok's talent. As graduation approached, Ashok was hot property and every company was vying to swoop him. Mr Rajan got placed in a top investment firm and Ashok went to work for a little known computer company named after a fruit.

Those were days before Facebook, mom, and Mr Rajan and Ashok lost touch. They hadn't met or seen each other for years. Mr Rajan told me he had recently come down to India for work and was chauffeured in the fancy company car. Kolkata being Kolkata, his car broke down and was taken to this upmarket garage. It was lunch time and most of the staff was out for lunch. A lone mechanic was disturbed but he seemed more than happy to help. As he finished his work, the mechanic caught a glimpse of the man inside the Mercedes. 'Rajan?' the mechanic said. Mr Rajan couldn't believe his eyes. It was Ashok.

After working very briefly for Apple, Ashok realized that his true calling was something to do with cars. He decided to come back to India and developed some major component for car engines. He sold this for a bomb and opened this garage. He personally repairs cars that come in, aided by all his mechanics and he said that not a single day has gone by when he felt he had 'worked'.

As we were about to land, he recommended I see this little known movie called *About Schmidt*. He said he feels the same way the lead character felt.

I managed to watch *About Schmidt* that very night. It starts with Schmidt's last day at work. He is sixty and has just retired. He was the VP of a very prestigious company. He suddenly looks back at his life and wonders how he got stuck in the usual rut and not once thought what he really wanted. He had graduated from Harvard, got hired, got married and wondered why he didn't take just one day out of all these days to think what he really wanted and work towards it.

As he was leaving, Mr Rajan said, 'I'm sixty and I'm very rich and at a very high position in a very big company. Looking back I can say I've achieved everything that everyone else wanted me to achieve.'

'And you know mom, what his parting words were?'

'I've not lived a life I wanted to live. I've lived someone else's life.'

And with that I finally ended my story. There was complete silence now. Mum's tears had rolled back in.

'Ma, I don't want to be Mr Rajan. I don't want to live a life like his.'

'But why didn't you tell me earlier about this business of yours?' she said in her post-crying voice.

'Because ma, I knew you would stop me from doing it.'

'Why would I stop you, beta?'

'Because that's what parents do, right? They don't want their son to take any risks.'

'Obviously beta, you know how much Papa and I have sacrificed for you. And why? Because Papa had started his business too, na? We know how difficult it is and we don't want you to suffer.'

'But ma, if every parent were to think like this, how would we have any entrepreneurs in this country? If Azim Premji's mum had said the same thing to him, who would have given Rohit a job?'

'I know beta…'

'Ma, I really love doing this. This is our idea, our business. I want to see it grow. I can't think about anything else, all day long the only thing on my mind is Alma Mater. All the time

I'm thinking of what do we do next? How to market this and how to get more stock? And a million other things like this. This is my life, ma. Please don't take this away from me.'

'Beta, would I stop you from doing what you want?'

'That's because you're always listening to Anu Aunty for everything. Whatever she decides for me is final.'

'Who the hell is Anu Aunty to decide for you??' she shouted.

Woah. Wait. Was I hearing right? Even the minions got up from their slumber.

'Anu Aunty was only brought in because you were confused and I didn't know what to do.

She is no one to take decisions that concern you and your life. If you want to do this, then you will get to do this and no Anu Panu can say anything.'

Okay. I was dreaming. Had they fought or something?

'When you were in the first standard, you wanted this automatic car. Papa's financial position was not too strong then and we didn't have the money for that. But I could never say no to you, so I sold my old bangles and bought you the car. You think I would ever stop you from being happy?'

And with that one sentence she brought tears to my eyes. They say your mother is the closest to God you can ever get and that moment sealed it forever for me. I couldn't take it anymore and ran and hugged her and we cried for a long time. A grown boy finds it really hard to communicate his feelings especially to his mother. It's not like we don't love them or anything, we just don't know how to express it. Most mothers take it in a wrong way and think their boys don't love them anymore. But we do, it's just that we can't say it. If only we boys could express ourselves. I didn't let my mum go and continued hugging her. I then slept in her lap just like I used to when I was a boy. This is what I needed I guess. I wanted my mum's love back.

Call me a sissy but I love my mom.

The minions couldn't take it anymore and burst into their own cries hugging each other. This made me highly suspicious of Lalit who was clearly using this opportunity for putting kai on Sivamma.

'Putting kai' is a term which refers to an interest shown by a member of the male community in a member of the female community with a possibility of love later on.

At Last it Happened!

The next day I got a call early in the morning from Mal. That was quite surprising because he knew I don't usually wake up that early.

'Rise and shine, bro.'

'Ahhh, what time is it?'

'Doesn't matter, it's time to move the boxes out of Sid's.'

'To where?'

'To our new office, bro.'

'What? Where?'

'Your house.'

Yup, my mother had just waived her magic wand. She had given us the garage to store all our stock. We got to use Lalit as our office boy temporarily and my little room became our first office. We were now officially a 'garage company'. I guess you really have to show your parents that you're passionate about something. That's when they're going to believe in you.

I logged on to Facebook a few days later to check up on what everyone was up to.

Notifications:

Aahana Thapar sent you a cow using Farmville.

Aahana Thapar sent you a dog using Farmville.

Aahana Thapar sent you a pig using Farmville.

Aahana Thapar sent you a pillow fight request.

Aahana Thapar commented on your photo.

Aahana Thapar commented on your photo.

2 friend requests:

When I checked the friend requests, something happened.

Have you experienced moments when a soundtrack starts playing in your mind? It could be like a song from a movie or a favourite song which sums up the entire moment? That was just happening to me. Reason: Devika had just added me as a friend!

Devika. Can you believe that? The girl I had been trying to add as a friend for all my life had just added me on Facebook. I wish I had words. She even added a note along with the friend request.

'Heya, aren't you the Alma Mater guy? My cousin bought a Cottonian hoodie from you guys. When are you gonna make some for Sophia High alumni? Love the concept by the way ☺'

She had even added a smiley.

My hands trembled as I clicked on the 'Yes' button to accept her friendship. This couldn't actually be happening. I pinched myself, then slapped myself twice, just to be sure. This meant I had full access to her profile. You know how much that means to a guy?

Okay, fine, that was a little creepy, but that was how it was.

I instantly replied to her query.

'Very soon, Devika. So you were in Sophia's eh? Which year?'

Of course I knew she was in Sophia's, she had passed out in 2004, she was working with O&M (Ogilvy and Mather) and she had a tattoo on her lower back. I knew all of this and way more. But I had to play it cool.

From that moment on, my life was divided into two parts. The first was obviously Alma Mater and the second was all about waiting for Devika to reply.

Part 3

Gujju Boy Strikes Back

A month had passed. It was now October and our website was still not done. The coding was taking longer than expected and Mal and I were getting really impatient. But our site was not a very simple one. Though the design looked simple, the back-end was pretty complicated. Our developer had given us mid-November as the date when the site or rather our e-commerce store would be ready.

I hadn't told the boys, except Sid, about the company yet. Though they'd be really pissed with me for spilling the beans so late, it had to be done. Besides, I was too eager to know what was happening with Shivani. I met the boys for lunch at Koshy's.

Koshy's is one of Bangalore's oldest grub joints. Going to the restaurant is like stepping back into the '70s. From delicious steaks to wonderfully sweet coffee, they've been serving it up for a long time now. Koshy's is the place where you go with your favourite book on a Sunday afternoon and read it with a cup of hot cappuccino.

Sid reached at the same time as me. As we finally found a place to sit, I tried to get the latest gossip about Shivani from him.

'Yo! what's happening with the Shivani scene?'

'Dude, bad scene man. I think she's gonna tell Rohit.'

'What? How do you know?'

'She said she loved Rohit too much now and was feeling guilty,' he said looking very dejected.

'Shit, seriously?'

'Yeah, bro, some bad times ahead.'

'Dude, but this happened before Rohit asked her out, right?'

'You think Rohit's gonna care a fuck about that?'

'But why are you still messaging her? Just tell him you are sorry.'

'Sorry won't bring a dead man alive, dude.'

Rohit and Mehtu entered and were visibly excited about the news I had to offer.

'Bro, I saw, I saw!' Rohit exclaimed.

'Saw what?' I said.

'Devika, dude. It fucking showed on my news feed. "Varun is now friends with Devika."'

'Ooooo,' everyone in unison.

Didn't I tell you guys this Oooo thingy happens.

'So tell, tell.'

'OK guys, I haven't called you guys to talk about Devika, there's something else.'

'What is it?'

'GMAT?'

'You got a job?'

'No you fucks. Have you been noticing people wearing those Cottonian and Josephite hoodies?'

'Dude, I know. That shit is cool. Where do you get those from? I got to get one man,' Rohit started rambling.

'Okay, so well...that's a company I started with Mal.'

'Whaaat?' Rohit and Gujju Boy screamed in unison.

Everyone just stared at me for some thirty seconds.

'Yeah.'

'You fucker, you could have asked me no?' Rohit said.

'Dude, that's cool but what about getting a real job?' Gujju Boy enquired.

'That is my job guys,' I said.

'Dude, are you sure you want to do all this now? I mean you could do this later,' he was clearly not very impressed.

'Later when, dude? Like when you're thirty-five? You are twenty-two now, if you have to take any risks, this is going to be the time. I mean imagine you're thirty-five with kids and family, you wouldn't want to leave your job then, man. There would be too much at stake then, right?'

'Hmmm...'

'And surprisingly you were the first one to inspire me to do something on my own.'

'Me?'

Gujju Boy couldn't believe this compliment.

'Yeah dude, you. Remember in eighth standard you showed me this film *Dead Poets' Society*?'

'Yeah', he said.

'Remember "Carpe Diem", the line they keep using in the movie? You used to run around screaming that at the top of your voice. Seize the day, baby. Isn't that what life is all about?'

Gujju Boy fell quiet.

After a long silence he finally said, 'Quite right, man. Carpe Diem.'

Meanwhile, a fight was brewing at our table. While Gujju Boy and I were engrossed in our conversation, Rohit and Sid had begun to quarrel. Apparently, Sid had sent some messages to Shivani which Rohit had cunningly read.

'You bastard, you been texting Shivani?' demanded Rohit.

'Dude, she texted me first,' said Sid apologetically.

'I read your fucking messages. What were you telling her not to tell me?'

'Nothing, man.'

'I wanna know, you asshole.'

'Dude, you're paranoid.'

'Oh! I'm paranoid?'

'You're always paranoid.'

'You're a…'

'Guys, guys,' Gujju Boy interrupted the chaos. Wow. I was getting more impressed with him by the minute. I mean until now he was always the behind-the-scenes kind of guy.

'I have to tell you guys something,' he said in a confessional tone.

Oh no. Don't tell me he is gay. Please god, please.

'Rohit, I'm sorry man.'

'Sorry for what?' Rohit was puzzled.

'I just couldn't keep it inside me anymore.'

'What?'

'Dude Rohit...'

'Yes, Gujju Boy...'

'I made out with Shivani.'

There are two things I can't forget to this day. One, the look on Rohit's face. But more importantly, the look on Sid's face.

Two days later, and thankfully, Rohit broke up with Shivani. Well, for obvious reasons.

Ping! Let the Cash Register Ring!

November 2009 was finally here and it was the 20th, which was super close to our website launch. Sadly, Devika and I had stopped messaging each other on FB. I guess the conversation got way too boring for her and our talks died a natural death.

While my heart was aching for some love, the development for the website was done. All that remained to do now was testing the website. We had to make sure we tested this thing thoroughly because it was an e-commerce store and it involved cash transactions. The last thing you want are any grumpy customers due to malfunctioning of the website.

The layout of our store was pretty simple. You choose the city you belong to, select your school or college and click on it. On clicking, for example, Bishop Cotton Boys' School, you'd be taken to a new page. This page consisted of all the merchandise that we had to offer to the alumni of Bishop Cotton. It included hoodies and tees for now. But we planned to add mugs, caps, stickers etc. a month later.

Once the customers are on the page they simply select the product they want. They then get re-directed to a check-out page where they simply enter their contact details and choose the payment option. As already mentioned earlier, we were very particular about the payment option because not everyone has a credit card or not everyone is comfortable using a credit card online. That's where the Cash on Delivery option comes in. So basically, you complete your order online and pay for it when you receive it at home. Old school style. You may think this method has a lot of drawbacks and a lot of people may return the packages. But thankfully, our return rate is just 7 per cent which is an industry standard. That means, for every hundred Cash on Delivery orders, only seven come back.

Mal and I sat with Devesh, the development manager at Exit and started testing our e-commerce store. We did multiple check-outs, bought all kinds of different items and tested the site at all possible levels. Whenever a customer wishes to buy using a credit card he is re-directed to the CC Avenue page. CC Avenue is like a middleman between Alma Mater and the customer and facilitates credit card transactions. CC Avenue is one of the most popular payment gateways in India and a vast majority of e-commerce stores use it as their payment gateway and they take 3–7 per cent on every transaction as commission.

Once a customer completes the transaction, he gets an email from us which is basically an invoice summarizing the order. Whenever an order is confirmed, the back-end team (which is only Mal and I for now) give Lalit the order sheet and address. Lalit packs the goods in the courier packet and every evening Aramex comes to pick it up. The customer gets his delivery usually within five working days. Even if he is in Timbaktoo.

'Boys, this is looking good, eh?' Devesh said, proud of his creation.

'Yup, Devesh. This is really neat,' we said together.

'Ah. There are some bugs here and there, so by 23 November this should be ready to go.'

Wow. This was it. 23 November. The day when everything would become official and our e-commerce store would be launched. I really couldn't believe we had come this far. Our small little idea born at Noon Wines was now going to go out to the world!

The days leading up to the website launch were really hectic. We had to get some basic systems in place quickly.

Firstly, we got all the stock arranged in a more structured manner. Orders would be coming in everyday and the last thing we wanted was us spending the entire day trying to find a particular tee or hoodie. I mean we had sizes ranging from XS to XXL in four different colours. So there was a lot of stock.

Secondly, we got all the courier packets ready. Now buying these packets from a regular stationery shop was going to cost a bomb so we had to go to the source i.e. the wholesaler. These boys sit in Chickpet, one of the most famous markest of Bangalore. So the packets that you get for ₹11 in a regular stationery shop you get for ₹4.50 from the Chickpet boys. It was more than a bargain. Since we were already in Chickpet, we bought all our office stationery as well. Marker pens, boxes of plain paper, printer cartridges, pens, tape and everything else a small company would need.

My desktop became the official office computer. This computer would be used for all office- related activities. Printing the invoice of the orders, checking up on the status of the orders etc.

I had to clean out all my porn though.

We fixed basic timings for all operations. The orders for the day will be checked at 3 p.m. every day, the order details would be handed over to Lalit at 5 p.m. Lalit, Mal and I would begin the packing and by 7 p.m. it would get done. The Aramex guy would come at 7.30 p.m. to pick up the packets.

Now let's do a mental checklist:

Website – Tick

Courier Partners – Tick

Courier Packets – Tick

Stock – Tick

Operations – Tick

Lalit – Tick

Porn Clean-up – Tick

Marketing – Nope

The last, but the most important aspect of it all. However, I had been doing my homework on that all this while and it was time to get the marketing strategy going.

Let There be Facebook!

It was 2009 and a revolution in the world of marketing was taking place. That revolution was Facebook. It made it possible for start-ups and smaller brands to market themselves in the same league as the big shots. Small brands could now put a word out about themselves for little or no money.

The first and most important thing is to obviously have a Facebook page. Since Mal and I had started Alma Mater, all our friends would obviously join our page and that would help us get others to join our page as well. For example, Vikram, a friend of mine joined the Alma Mater page. The fact that Vikram joined my page would show up on all his friends' news feed. If Vikram had five hundred friends on FB, a lot of them would come to know that he had joined our page. Seeing this, some of his friends will then join our page and the process would repeat with other people as well.

Facebook was not only becoming a new means of marketing, it was becoming the future of marketing.

If I were to make it simpler—till now there was no possible way of saying anything wrong about a brand or a company. Sure you didn't like a burger at McDonalds or the service at KFC, you could tell you friends about it or write to the papers. That's it. A very crucial example that illustrates this point is: Some time back, a couple of Domino's employees posted a video of themselves contaminating pizzas at a local Domino's outlet. The video was uploaded on Youtube and went viral and got a crazy number of views. The brand faced a lot of criticism and it could have led to something bigger. But Domino's had a huge FB presence which restricted the damage to a huge extent. An immediate video was posted using the response feature on Youtube which got an equal number of views and that quickly suppressed the situation. Had Domino's not had any Facebook, Twitter or Youtube presence, we can only wonder what that would have done to the brand.

Similarly, a leading lock-making firm in China considered themselves too big for social media. A few bloggers posted how their locks could be opened with just a ball point pen. With no presence whatsoever on Facebook or Twitter, word quickly spread and the company was brought to its knees. I think every one of their employees is now on Facebook after that.

It's not just the big brands but smaller brands too which can benefit from Facebook. You can market anything you want, quickly spread the word about your brand and do a lot more at no cost at all. I think starting a business has become easier than ever before. I know a friend of mine whose mother used to make these delicious homemade chocolates. I told her it's extremely important to get the word out on FB. After setting up and managing her page, her mother has quadrupled her sales all in two months.

So, for an internet business like Alma Mater there was only one thing to do. And that was Facebook. And you know what the best part is? It's FREE.

Now when you're starting a Facebook page, there are two very important things that can help viral your brand name. Images and Videos. Everyone loves seeing pictures and everyone loves watching videos. If you can make this the core of your page the numbers will automatically come.

We already had some awesome looking hoodies, what we needed now were a bunch of pretty girls to pose in them. Everyone loves seeing pictures of pretty girls including girls themselves. I was already an avid photographer so it was time to start making some calls and arranging for the Alma Mater models.

So I called my friends, who called their friends and eventually we were able to get a lot of pretty girls to pose for our hoodies. What was amazing was the fact that the girls were actually really excited about posing because they thought of us as a cool brand.

And also the fact that I was one awesome photographer and we gave them free hoodies.

While I really love taking photographs, it gets a bit interesting when it comes to clicking girls.

1) 'OMG, Varun, no. Have you seen me in pics, ya? I'll ruin all your shots.'

So firstly, the girls insist that they are not pretty enough or photogenic enough for the photographs. You have to move mountains to convince them otherwise they wouldn't budge.

2) 'Yuck. I look sooo bad in this one. You can't put this up.'

The second major hurdle is that they are never, ever satisfied with any of the photographs. Words like 'yuckk', 'chee', 'barf' are used generously. No matter how well the shot has come out, a single line seems to speak for all of them—'I look so fat in this one.'

3) 'Okay, I wanna see how I look ya.'

A really popular problem. They have to see each shot after it's taken. Come rain, hail, snow or whatever, they have to see the photo. Once they do please refer to the point above.

4) 'Okay, you have to send me the pics before putting them up.'

So once they are sent, there's usually a common reply. Again, refer to point number 2.

Finally, you have no choice but to upload the photographs, right? Once they do get uploaded and published and show up everywhere, that's when the comments and the likes start flowing.

They amass numerous likes and numerous comments and obviously the picture is upgraded to the high status of a profile picture. The best part is that the girls keep checking the comments every second but respond to them only a few days later to act like they don't care at all. Eventually the girls thank all the admirers and everyone is happy.

So by 22 November we had this awesome collection of photographs of guys and girls posing with our hoodies and tees. The latter being the majority. The interesting thing was these were ex-students of the school for which they had posed, a fact which would help us greatly on Facebook later on. I mailed Seema all the pictures we had taken and she arranged them on our website in a beautiful way. If our website looked good till now, with all those product shots it looked even better.

Your Son is a Salesman?

The day assigned for the launch of the website was only twenty-four hours away and my mum didn't know how to answer all those curious relatives and friends of hers. I mean how are these people going to understand an e-commerce business? And this was back in 2009 when it was still in its infancy in India. For them, I was nothing but a T-shirt salesman and that funnily depressed my mum. So when an old friend of hers called her up, the conversation went something like this.

'Hi Poornima, long time no?'

'I know ya, how have you been?'

'Good ya, how's Varun?'

'He is doing some work ya. What's Aparna doing?'

'Oh, she is working with Goldman Sachs. They just promoted her, you know. She is thinking of going for an MBA also. To America. Oh, I can't wait to start looking for her.'

'Arre wah! I'm so proud of Appu… (mum is not actually). Why don't you bring her home sometime?

'I will, I will. But what is our Varun up to?'

This is what my mom *wanted* to say. 'Oh, your daughter is working for Goldman Sachs? My son is working for Microsoft in USA. Ha ha. Beat that.'

However, this is what she said: 'He is selling T-shirts ya.'

'What are you saying, Poornima? Selling T-shirts?'

'Yes.' (depressed)

'Is Varun a salesman, Poornima?'

(Almost going to cry), 'Something like that ya...'

'Haw. What are you saying? I can't believe this.'

'I don't know what to do. Who will marry him now?' Anyway, thanks for calling, ya.'

I guess we are all salesmen at some level. Everyone in this world is trying to sell something. Be it a service, product, goods or anything else. In fact, even Aparna is actually a salesman. On a different level. The question is not whether you're a salesman or not. Are you better than the other salesman?

D-Day—Well, Almost

It was 23 November. The day of our website launch had finally arrived. This was the day Mal and I have been waiting for for a long time. We had gone through a lot of shit to get to this point and looking back, I'm very surprised that it had actually come.

We kept making frantic calls to Devesh throughout the day to monitor the progress of the site. Meanwhile, I had created the Facebook page for Alma Mater. It was just a basic page with no pictures or information as yet. We only wanted to add all of that once the site was launched.

We called everyone we could think of and told them about the website. We also got a call from our manufacturer that day asking for his money. We gave him the good news that the site was finally going to be launched enabling regular sales. We assured him that he would get his money in a week's time.

We started creating a lot of buzz on our profile page too. All our friends had the Alma Mater logo as their profile picture so there was a lot of excitement about our site. In the meantime, Devesh kept calling and giving us updates. My mum had told all her friends as usual and though no one understood this 'e-commerce business' there was a considerable buzz in the kitty party circle as well.

We were frantically making preparations for the launch when we again got a call from Devesh.

'Boys, bugs still there. Don't think we can launch today.' Devesh said over the phone.

Shit. All the hype and build-up and there are still some bugs. We had already informed and told everyone about the launch. This was going to be really embarrassing. We kept getting frantic emails from Devesh about the site crashing. We decided to be as close to ground zero as possible and we went straight to Exit Design again.

'Boys, some code has gone horribly wrong,' he said, breathing heavily.

'So?'

'No, I mean the entire site is crashing.'

Mal and I were no techies so we needed this simplified for us.

'It means we don't launch till issue sorted.'

'How long could that take, Devesh?'

'Ah, can't say.'

'At least give us a time frame...'

'Twenty days?'

Oh fuck. This was bad. This was really bad. We had to launch the website so we could start selling ASAP. The thing was, we had to pay our manufacturer and we had already passed the credit limit. We had maxed out all our loans and personal savings and this delay could spell doom for our company.

'Devesh, is there no way we could launch earlier?'

'No boys. We really fucked.'

That we were.

Mal and I went back to discuss this at our original company headquarters at Shiva's. We hadn't been there for some time now and seeing us, the boys couldn't control their happiness. They handed us our usual smoke and chai and we began contemplating what to do next.

'This is dicey, bro,' Mal said, obviously worried.

'Yup. Can we take more loans, Mal?'

'I've taken the maximum I could in my name.'

'Shit man, we're screwed. When do we have to give him the money by?'

'In a week, man. Can you arrange something?'

'I've already busted all my savings bro.'

Things were looking really gloomy now. We started calling all our friends to borrow some money, but we couldn't even gather half of what was needed. Mal decided to meet some bank people he knew and I even spoke to some of my uncles for some investment.

But we were two twenty-two-year-olds with no business experience. Nobody cared. Both of us returned empty-handed.

I was really down at that moment. All the hard work and pain and some stupid bug in the code had destroyed all of that. Our manufacturer had warned us about our payments and we knew there was definitely no way he would give us more time. Things couldn't have gotten worse.

Time passed at a snail's pace that day. There was actually nothing much to do so we went back to our respective homes. I then did what I used to do for a long time before this company started. I looked at my ceiling fan again and got lost in my thoughts.

'Why did this have to happen now? What wrong had we done? Why couldn't things be smooth? Maybe my mum was right. Doing a business is no easy thing. There are a lot of heartbreaks and this was definitely one of them'. Lost in these thoughts, a solitary tear ran down my cheek and that's when the phone rang again.

It was Devesh.

God, I hope there's no more bad news again.

'Baroon, Baroon,' he screamed

'Yes, Devesh.'

'Come to office. Fast.'

Oh shit. I instantly got dressed and left for Exit Design. I feared the worst and was really feeling the strain now. The pressure was getting to me and I was on the verge of cracking.

When I reached Exit Design along with Mal, we found Devesh neck deep in work on our website.

'Baroon, Roaannn… '

'We are on. We are on. All bug fixed. We launch.'

'We launch? When?'

'Now, now.'

I couldn't believe what I heard.

The team had been working doubly hard to get this thing going. Apparently a small code was written wrongly and that one line of code had caused all the issues.

'It's all done, Baroon and Roaaan. You go and launch. All the best.'

Karn, Seema and the rest of the team at Exit gave us their blessings and we ran back home to get this thing started.

It was 10 p.m. and we caught the first auto we could find.

'Boss, Koramangala?'

'Two hundred and twenty rupees.'

'Look boss, I have only seventy, you want to go?'

'No chance.'

I started walking away. He had no choice, so he screamed.

'Okay come, we go.'

D-Day Dawns

As soon as we reached home we started the launch process.

This included two major steps. We had a list of five thousand people to whom we would send out an emailer informing them about the start of our site.

And the second and most important thing—launching our Facebook page. As soon as the pictures of those guys and pretty girls wearing our hoodies showed up on the news feed, people were bound to check out our website.

So I quickly sent out those emails and began work on the Facebook page. I uploaded all the pictures, put out all the information and hit the PUBLISH button.

The Alma Mater Facebook page was now officially live.

The Alma Mater website was now officially live.

At exactly 11.15 p.m. on 23 November 2009, we got our first order. It was for a Cottonian hoodie, size L.

Things went insane that night. In the matter of minutes we had seventy-five fans already. The number kept increasing by leaps and bounds. In fact, the entire night Mal and I were on the phone checking our Facebook page. Each time we checked it, the numbers increased and so did the rate at which our heart was beating.

The orders kept pouring in as did the congratulatory emails. Everyone knew about Alma Mater now and there was no stopping it. That night alone we got seventy-five orders and the Facebook page wouldn't stop buzzing. People kept posting on it, congratulating us and everyone kept telling us that something like this should have happened a long time ago. There was obviously a clear market for this.

Why this Kolaveri Di?

I couldn't sleep all night and kept answering all the emails, the queries, the Facebook messages—it was chaos. At 2.30 a.m. I got a call from Sid. What the hell did he want at this time?

'Bro, congrats for the website,' he said.
'Sid, thanks man. What's happening? All cool I hope.'
'Uh, yeah.'
'Dude?'
No response.
'Dude, what's going on?' I asked again.
'Bro, you're gonna hate me.'
'What happened?'
'Bro, I had gone to Cirrus yesterday and I was really drunk. I mean I was really gone. I met Devika there.'
'My Devika?'
'Yeah man…and…'
'And what, you fuck? Tell me.'

'Dude, I told her how you were stalking her. I even told her about the tattoo. Dude, I'm really sorry man, I didn't mean it, I was extremely drunk and it all spilled out. I'm extremely sorry, bro.

Fuck. Fuck. Fuck.

I couldn't say anything to that. I slammed the phone down. I felt really sick, I couldn't even imagine what she must be thinking of me. I decided to quickly send her a Facebook message to calm things down but the damage was done. She had deleted me from her friend list. Not only that, she had imposed very strict privacy settings which meant I couldn't even search for her profile. I can't describe how I felt at that moment.

I decided to delete Sid from my life.

Meanwhile, things were going crazy with Alma Mater helping me take my mind off this.

I was up the entire night and the numbers kept growing. Our Facebook page was getting viral and the orders kept coming in.

The next day, as planned, we checked the confirmed orders from the back-end. Printouts of the orders and invoice were taken and we began the packing along with Lalit. The orders were diverse and from all parts of the country. One guy had ordered from Delhi, another from Mumbai, there were a lot from Bangalore and again I kept thinking, would all this have been possible had we opened just a physical store somewhere? We just about managed to finish the packing by 7.30, and as expected the Aramex guy came for pick-ups. And with that our first official shipment went out.

Magic Numbers

The night of 24 November was just as frantic. The emails continued to pour in and our fan count had gone up to three hundred in the matter of one day. I uploaded some more photographs we had shot and noticed that each time we uploaded some pictures, the fan count on our Facebook page shot up like crazy. Since pictures were doing the trick for us, it was obvious they had to be networked well, i.e., they had to reach more number of people than the current crowd.

And thankfully, Facebook had invented a beautiful little concept called 'tagging'. So this is what I did. I took a photograph of a guy wearing a Cottonian hoodie and tagged all the Cottonians I knew on it. Ideally, when someone tags you in pictures and if you're not in them, it annoys the crap out of you. But here some guy was wearing a Cottonian hoodie and the guy tagged was also a Cottonian. So he wouldn't get that annoyed (or at least we believed so). Thus, I started maxing out the numbers of tags on each picture, which is fifty.

No sooner had we done that, the Facebook page started going viral, which meant more hits for our website. That was because when one guy gets tagged in a picture, most of his five hundred friends see it. However, when fifty guys get tagged on a picture, this information potentially goes out to five thousand people. That's the magic of Facebook. The power to reach as many people as you want without spending a single rupee.

Another factor that worked for us was the presence of all these pictures on the walls of alumni groups on Facebook. Every school or college has its own group or page on Facbook and we started posting our pictures on these groups like crazy.

The result—one thousand fans in the matter of three days. Yup, one thousand fans of a hitherto unknown company.

While I was busy with all of this, Sid kept calling me but I didn't take his call. I didn't give a damn actually. He had broken the cardinal rule of friendship. Gujju Boy and Rohit kept urging me to at least talk to him but I wouldn't listen. I didn't want to see his face or talk to that idiot.

Angel in Disguise?

While my love life and friendship were completely screwed, things at Alma Mater were going off the hook. Since we started, schools from all over the country were contacting us to add themselves on our site. However, we still needed signed permission from every one of them and that took a lot of time. Initially, we had only four schools and one college and the alumni of these schools could visit our site and buy their stuff. But the students from other schools and colleges loved our merchandise so much, they wanted similar stuff for themselves too.

Thus, though we were not ready for it, we had to launch phase two of our business plan just weeks after launching the Alma Mater e-store. Phase two of the plan was bulk order.

This basically meant an arrangement through which you could order hoodies or tees for your class or batch. We would customize it for you in any colour and print any designs for you. We got our first big order within days of launching this option on our site. It was for hoodies for the entire tenth stdandard batch of Baldwin Girls' High School. It was a big order and it pretty much set the precedent for our business. We were still getting our operations in place for the bulk order system as it involved a lot of logistical planning, especially with our manufacturer. Also, we didn't take any small orders then and the minimum number for placing a bulk order with us at that time was hundred. Our delivery timeline was usually twenty-five to thirty days, which was quite a lot.

So we knew from the very start we had to take care of two very important things. Reduce the number of days for the bulk order, and more importantly, reduce the time required for delivery.

Another interesting thing happened within days of launching our site. We got an email from a person asking us to call him urgently as he wanted to discuss something with us. I thought it was just another email from some customer for a query, so I gave him a call.

'Hi, This is Varun calling from Alma Mater. You had sent us an email?' I said.

'Yeah Varun, nice to hear from you. I saw your website. Great idea and great brand. Wanted to sit and talk with you guys.' The man sounded young and enthusiastic.

'But what is this regarding?' I said.

'Well, I'm a venture capitalist and I invest in start-ups. I find your company very promising and I want to make a serious investment.'

My heart almost stopped beating.

'Wow, that's great, Sir,' I was gobsmacked for words.

'So could we meet?'

'Of course,' I said unable to control my excitement.

That's the unbelievable thing about starting your company. Every day is not only a new and different day, it's an exciting opportunity. You get goosebumps when you get off the phone with a complete stranger who wants to invest serious money in your company.

So we met the investor the next day at a posh Bangalore hotel. For once I wasn't dressed in my track pants. We spoke about various things and we told him our story—how we started, our future plans, etc. He was mighty impressed and was really keen on investing in us but the problem was that we were not ready yet. I mean we had just started and our company didn't even have a decent valuation.

A VC or venture capitalist could be one of the most important people in your life if you have started a company. He/she invests in your company for an equity or stake. Our company had just taken off, which meant we weren't worth a lot. So say if we were worth ₹100 now, he could take 20 per cent of our company and give us ₹20. But if we waited for a year and built our brand well, then we would be worth at least ₹1000 and for the same 20 per cent he would end up paying ₹200. Made sense, right? Besides, we didn't need the money now anyway. Our sales were funding us for now but we would need additional capital soon.

So we called our investor the next day and thanked him for showing interest in us. We told him we weren't ready to be funded as yet but would definitely think of it in the future. Besides, we were still learning new things every single day and wanted to know everything about running this business before a VC came on board.

Goodbye Anu Aunty?

Alma Mater was now getting famous and a lot of people were talking about it. Seeing so many people come home to buy the goods, my mum went from being depressed to super happy. She finally understood this T-shirt business of mine and was showing signs that she was proud of me. A lot of customers who came to my house would talk to my mum and congratulate her. After a gap of nearly three months, Anu Aunty finally paid us a visit.

'Poo, heya. Such a long tiiime,' she said, flinging her Commercial Street Gucci rip-off on our sofa.

'Anooo,' my mum said and they hugged each other like long-lost sisters.

'How's everything ya?' Anu Aunty asked.

'Same old only, ya. But you tell, how are things?' said my mother.

'Good ya, Poo. Oh! Did I tell you Arjun got a promotion?'

'Wow! This calls for a treat, Anu.'

Actually, mum was not even remotely happy about Arjun getting a promotion.

'Ha ha, surely Poo, anything for you. Arre, where's Varun, how's he?' said Anu Aunty.

'Oh he is good, Poo. I've never seen him happier,' my mother said.

'Is he still selling T-shirts?' Aunty's eyes widened in horror.

'It's an e-commerce store, Anu.'

Wow. I was so proud of my mum that day.

'Kya?' Anu Aunty snickered.

'E-commerce Anu, some internet thing.'

'What internet thing ya, he is a T-shirt salesman.'

'Anu, not a T-shirt salesman, but an entrepreneur.'

'He he. If you say so...' Anu Aunty giggled.

'Arre, at least Varun is bold enough to do this, what has Arjun done?' my mother said.

Woah. What's this?

'He just got promoted Poo, and is going to America for MBA.' Anu Aunty looked ready for battle.

'What Varun is doing is also good. You know how many kids come here and keep thanking me?' my mother said.

'You should tell him to stop this stupidity. Running a business is not for these youngsters. He is trying to act much bigger than his boots ya. You're ignorant, Poo.'

'No Anu, *you're* ignorant. You comment on things without even knowing what they mean.'

'Pch, now you're getting angry, accha let's change the topic.'

They did change the topic that day but something else changed. My mum no longer thought of me as an underachiever anymore. She understood what I was doing and completely supported that. I loved my mum and her support meant the world to me.

Alma Matters

The greatest thing about starting Alma Mater was all those emails and appreciation we got from our customers. I remember we got an email in the early days from a gentleman from Bishop Cotton from the batch of 1956. He said that wearing the Cottonian hoodie reminded him of all those wonderful years spent at school and even though that was such a long time ago, he still got goosebumps when he thought of the days spent in school. But the most interesting email we got was from an ex-Cottonian from New Jersey. He had bought a Cottonian sweatshirt from us. He happened to visit this coffee shop near his office in New Jersey and was amazed to find another guy wearing a Cottonian sweat. He immediately walked up to him and they got talking. Both of them realized they were just two batches apart and had a lot of common friends living in the same area whom they never knew about. More importantly, they became friends. I guess that is exactly what we were looking to create through Alma Mater.

Another great kick we got out of this entire thing was to actually see someone wearing our hoodie or tee at a random place. When we first started the company, we were spotting people almost on a daily basis. In fact, I once saw this kid wearing one of our hoodies walking down Brigade road. I instantly stopped him and took a picture. I still have that photo. Later, when Mal had gone for a holiday to Goa, he saw some guys wearing our hoodies there too. Our fans on Facebook sent us messages that they saw people wearing our stuff in London, New York, Los Angeles, Tokyo and some vague city in Germany even!

I remember, when we were in school, there was a sense of pride associated with wearing the uniform. I guess once I passed out of school, I really missed that. School had given me a sense of belonging and we really wanted to re-create that. Till date we get emails and phone calls from ex-students when they receive their sweatshirts or T-shirts, telling us how they love them and how a simple T-shirt has brought back those golden memories.

They are students both young and old. Some who passed out in the '50s and '60s and some just recently. One thing is common to all of them—the pride and love for their Alma Mater.

Part 4

'Varun, Get the Hell Out of my House'

Five months had passed since we had started Alma Mater. We were slowly getting established in the market. We had added five more schools in Bangalore and secured a school from Ooty and two more from Chennai. Our operation was now spreading across South India and we were growing at a considerable rate. The way we conducted our business was changing.

Remember, I had spoken about how it was very important for us to consolidate our bulk order business? Well, we were finally able to work out the logistics with our manufacturer. Using the new system, we had brought down the minimum quantity required to make customized merchandise to thirty-five. Also, the timeline was reduced to twenty days. This was a far cry from the early days. We were now getting a lot of bulk orders from all over the country which was contributing to the bulk of our turnover. We had also started shipping internationally and had shipped our hoodies to London, New York, Boston, Berlin, and to as far as Australia and New Zealand.

I still hadn't spoken to Sid and Devika still hadn't relaxed her privacy settings. The group was now divided and I hung out with Rohit and Gujju Boy only when Sid wasn't around. He did try a lot to reconcile but I just couldn't get myself to forgive him.

Arjun had gotten yet another promotion and Anu Aunty was in seventh heaven again. She still called me a salesman and continued as the head of the kitty party circuit.

Mal and I had just concluded our first official business trip. We went to Chennai and Mumbai to tap more schools there. We were now expanding and my house was getting too small for all of us.

The time was ripe to start looking for a new office because my mum, though proud of me now, was not particularly happy with the way things were going.

'Varun, get the hell out of my house.'

Those were the exact words uttered by my mom one fine day, which forced us to get off our asses and look for an office. Well, until then, we were a typical garage company and we had no worries in the world. The distance between my office and my bed was six feet and the kitchen was down the corridor. Life was all rosy but little did I know that trouble was silently brewing outside.

We had not only outgrown the garage, but also the house! It was a mad scene—stock coming and going, clients constantly knocking on the door, pretty girls flowing in to pose for our hoodies, vendors calling constantly and, in the middle of all of this was me, in my pajamas, enjoying every moment of it. Just when I was planning to take over the house, I got an ultimatum from my mom. We were asked to move out, else I would have to find a new home to live in. So we got off the couch and called Justdial again. And like before, Justdial came to our rescue and helped us in finding a new office.

I was loath to leave the house. Working in my bed, Lalit's pakodas and tea to curb the stress, my terrace where every single Alma Mater photo shoot had happened, getting up at eleven in the morning, and a lot of other things had to be left behind. But I hoped the new office would bring in a lot of new possibilities.

We no longer were a garage company and things were going to get serious. I figured it was for the best but nothing can beat the fun of running your company from your own garage. On a serious note, you learn most aspects of your business in your garage, when it's small and manageable. This helps you to constantly think of the next step and figure out ways to scale up, especially when you know you're going to get evicted.

Anu Aunty and Branding

Like I mentioned before, even though I hate kitty parties, they have actually helped me a lot in my business. When it comes to creating a brand, you and I have unknowingly imbibed so much information from kitty parties and aunties that it all comes together when you set out to do something on your own.

Take good ol' Anu Aunty, for example. For ages I have watched her brag about her son, Arjun, and his accomplishments. Wherever she went, there would be just one thing on her mind—Arjun. What she did was, indirectly create a brand. A brand that all the aunties around trusted and wanted their sons to be like, and a brand they wanted their daughters to now marry. She sold Brand Arjun like there was no tomorrow and nothing can take that away. Brand Arjun would be the toast of every kitty party and the topic of conversation among all the moms at the PTA, even though he was the biggest sissy I'd ever known.

So, I had indirectly learnt a lot about branding from Anu Aunty and kitty parties. When we started Alma Mater, I'd constantly talk about it to everyone like crazy. I practically lived in my Cottonian hoodie and would be seen walking around wearing it everywhere (Mum stopped serving me dinner unless I took it off). Whoever I would meet, I would tell them about Alma Mater and go on and on. It did help me start off but then there was something else—the mother of all kitty parties—Facebook. Now a kitty party is basically a place where aunties gather to gossip incessantly. The gossip would spread, and soon everyone would hear about it and start talking about it. Facebook, as you all know, is very similar.

Now a lot of my friends feel a tad shy about promoting their 'brands' shamelessly. Like Mum never promoted me in any of the kitty parties (I didn't give her a reason to do so) and hence, I was considered a black sheep among the aunties. A zero brand, basically. So it all comes down to how well you sell yourself and create a brand. We keep our fans on our Facebook page posted about every single activity in our company just like Anu Aunty does in the case of Arjun. We are so shameless, we tag random people in our photos and show up on everyone's wall uninvited. Indirectly, everyone starts talking about it and well—the seeds of a brand are sown.

So, if as a kid you were swindled into attending one of those most annoying kitty parties by your mother, then it might just pay off in the future and save you some money.

Hey Bro!

Since we started Alma Mater, a lot of interesting events happened where we couldn't help but smile. One of them happened over the phone once.

You see, we do a lot of work over the phone and we get numerous calls every day. The calls could be to place orders or make some enquiries, stuff like that. But one call still stands out as compared to the rest. This happened when we initially started the company. A girl called me up asking for a hoodie.

'Hello, Alma Mater?' she said.

'Yes', I said.

'I wanted to, like, order a hoodie.'

'For sure...what size and colour?'

'Okay, so a black, small.'

'Great...I'll get it shipped.'

'Uh, you don't have to do that.'

'No, I have to ship it,' I said.

'I don't understand, why do you have to ship it?' she asked.

'How do I send it then?' I was a bit puzzled.

'Okay, so, you can send it by road. I live in Bangalore itself.'

The word 'shipping' is still interpreted wrongly. It simply means 'sending by courier' but the girl on the other end thought otherwise.

Another wonderful incident happened once when I was in a bookstore. I spotted a guy standing near me wearing one of our hoodies. I decided to strike a conversation with him and was completely shocked by what he said.

Me: 'Hey man, where did you get that hoodie from?'

Guy: 'Why do you wanna know, bro?'

Me: 'Simply dude. Wanted to pick up one.'

Guy: 'My comp makes these, bro.'

Me: 'WHAT? WHAT COMP?'

Guy: 'My company, bro.'

Me: 'Dude, are you sure?'

Guy: 'Yeah, bro. Full sure.'

Me: 'What's the name of the comp?'

Guy: 'Alma bro.'

Me: 'Alma Mater? You're Varun?'

Guy: 'No, bro. Those guys are just the face of the comp.'

Me: 'Oh.'

Guy: 'Yeah, bro. Who has the time to market and shit, bro? Got the whole comp set and got them to market, bro.'

Me: 'Oh, I didn't know.'

Guy: 'Bro, I'm running five different companies here. Can't take care of each. My main focus is real estate, bro. Made a killing there. Just picked up an Audi for Dad.'

Me: 'Faaak.'
Guy: 'Yeah, bro. Gotta run bro, girl is waiting.'
Me: 'Dude, but how do I get the hoodie?'
Guy: 'Call the office bro, number is on Facebook.'

Fast Forward

They say that all good things come to an end and something similar happened to me two months later. Well, for one, I still hadn't reconciled with Sid and that troubled me a lot; and the second, Alma Mater was growing at a fast pace and we needed some money to sustain that growth.

Since the company had started, we had put all our savings into it and had taken multiple loans. I mean the sales actually paid for the growth of the company. But now we didn't have any more money to invest and the time had come to approach a VC or an angel investor.

We had to expand the number of schools we were making products for and we also needed to better our bulk order business. Over the past two months, we had improved our systems and had brought down the minimum quantity to thirty and the delivery timeline to fifteen days. But we had to improve that, for which we needed money to keep enough inventory, to have a sales team, to hire more employees, to increase our marketing efforts, to have TV, radio and newspaper ads and to also increase our online ad spending. Like I have said before, people were willing to invest in us even when we had just started. We weren't ready then. But we now needed the investment, else our growth would suddenly come to a halt.

So both Mal and I began focusing on getting an investor on board. My mum who had initially supported the entire thing was again getting doubtful of our intentions. She figured we had slackened too much and it was very important to show her and the ever-intruding Anu Aunty that we had a real business at hand. Another major problem was that Mal had quit his job and his parents were not too happy with things as well. I mean, we had started a company and all that but we were still not drawing any salaries. So there was a lot of pressure from all sides and we had to do something quickly.

In the meantime, I had met the boys at Chung Wah for some good old Chinese food. We hadn't even finished the starters when something unexpected happened—Sid walked in. He coolly walked up and took his seat amongst us. Apparently, Rohit and Gujju Boy had invited him in hopes of a reconciliation.

'Isn't this great? All of us together again, aye?' Gujju Boy said, as if we had come for a family reunion.

I didn't say anything.

'This is reminding me of the good ol' days boys,' Rohit said, sounding like a male version of Oprah Winfrey.

I didn't say anything.

'So Varun, what say man, let's end this?' said Gujju Boy. I wanted to kill him any second now.

'C'mon dude,' said Rohit.

'C'mon man,' echoed Gujju Boy.

Sid didn't say anything till then. He then suddenly opened his fucking trap.

'Leave it guys. Who wants to be friends with an asshole who puts a girl before his childhood friend?' he said.

This time I lost it. I took a blind swing at Sid. He ducked and swung back at me.

The families around us were appalled. Some of them even closed their kids' eyes.

'You fucking bastard, get the fuck out of here,' I said.

'You get the fuck out,' replied Sid.

'I'm going. Guys you coming?' I announced.

No Response. WTF?

'Guys, you fucking coming or what?' I repeated.

No response.

Fuck them, I thought, and stormed out of there. I was so angry, I could have killed anyone. I walked up to an auto guy.

'Boss, fucking Koramangala,' I said.

'Ah Saar, two hundred please,' he said.

'Fifty you bastard, are you coming or not?'

The auto guy got so scared he took only forty from me when we reached there. When I finally got into my room, I realized the gravity of the situation. I had just left three of my closest friends behind. I had never felt lonelier than that moment in my whole life.

Show Me the Money

We needed some money from an investor in order to expand, but before that could happen, we needed to get the right valuation for our company. To add to that, pressure from Mom to suddenly do an MBA was building up. I couldn't understand this at all. The reason for this was very simple and also very stupid. As mentioned earlier, both Mal and I were not drawing any salaries from Alma Mater. All the money we made was put back into the company. So technically speaking, we were broke all the time. On the other hand, Arjun was now drawing a salary of fifty thousand a month.

In the coming days, Mal and I were finally able to lock down a good financial consultant by the name of Ram Madhvani to do our valuation. We went to his office and gave him all our financial details. He did a thorough survey of our company and said that he would try and find the right valuation. The only problem was that he was old fashioned and didn't understand the concept of e-commerce and its potential in this country in the next three years.

You need to get the right valuation before you find an investor to come on board. Based on the valuation of the company, the investor will pick up a stake ranging from 10 to 30 per cent.

Valuation basically means determining the worth of a company. It depends on a lot of parameters but mostly on the current turnover and projected growth at the end of three to five years.

We hoped the financial consultant would do some justice to our company because we had to grow and for that we needed some money soon.

Things at home were also not exactly pleasant. There were a lot of times when I still had to take money from my mom. This was obviously going to cause some tension and it was obvious that the cause of tension would be Anu Aunty. I woke up one morning and wasn't very surprised with the conversation between her and my mother.

'So Poo, tell me ya, how's Varoon's T-shirt thing going?'

'It's going well ya,' said my mother.

Anu Aunty could sense my mum's mood. She was born to do that.

'What happened, Poo?'

'Nothing ya.' My mother valiantly tried looking cheerful.

And then the token tear gave her true feelings away. Sigh. Just when I thought mum was on my side and I had driven Anu Aunty away forever.

'Tell no Poo, please ya,' Anu Aunty was beside herself with curiosity.

'What to tell, Anu? He still takes money from me,' said my mother.

'Haw, he doesn't give you money?'

'No ya, not yet.'

'That's sad ya, Poo. Arjun tho gives me the entire fifty thousand he earns ya,' Anu Aunty said smugly.

What else would that sissy Arjun do with the money?

'Poo, I'm telling you, this is a wrong thing for Varun to do ya. I don't think he can run his own business,' said Anu Aunty.

My mom started crying even louder.

'I'm telling you ya, Poo, these boys of today don't think only. You should tell Varun to stop this business-phisness at once.'

Mum's crying intensified and my anger and frustration at her swept over me. Et tu, mum? I grimaced.

'What to do, Anu? Now definitely no one is going to marry him,' my mother said.

That is the problem with the Indian Parents Society. They don't understand the concept of entrepreneurship. They don't understand that we had to get funded to take our business to the next level and once that happened, both Mal and I would actually make a lot of money ourselves. But everybody wants to think short-term, right?

I was also trying to call Rohit and Mehtu but both weren't taking my calls. To hell with those fuckers. If they want to be with that fuck Sid, then so be it. I would rather live this life without any friends than be with them.

The Great Depression

A few days had passed and our financial advisor finally called us for a meeting. His office was like a typical accountant's office. Lots of computers, lots of cubicles, telephones ringing constantly—basically complete chaos. We landed in his office and directly got to the point.

'So, Mr Ram, what is the verdict?' we asked in unison.

'Boys, I've been doing a lot of research about this e-commerce thing and I'm not very convinced,' he said.

'But Sir...'

Before we could say anything, he cut us off. 'You see boys, whatever said and done, there will still be only a small minority that would be interested in buying online.'

'Oh, we definitely don't think so Sir...' He cut us off again with a wave of his hand.

'It doesn't matter what you think, boys. It matters what I think. People in India are not very comfortable buying online' His tone was getting curt.

'But Sir, that's changing...,' I said.

'Guys, have you come here to teach me?' he said.

'Well, so, have you come up with a figure?' Mal asked.

'I have, but it's not very promising.'

And with that he threw the valuation papers at us. I had a bad feeling about this. My fears were confirmed once we read up all the numbers. This guy had screwed us over. He was pitching us at ₹75 lakh. This was not even our yearly turnover and he had simply predicted that the use of e-commerce would hardly grow in the next three years. This was almost a devaluation.

'Guys, there's not much of a future there,' said Mr Ram, looking grim.

'Mr Ram, what are you saying?' I said.

'That's the truth, boys.'

'Mr Ram... ' I got up from my chair and said, 'We have gone through shit in order to start this company. I put my life's savings into this and took a huge loan from my friends, and you can't even imagine how that feels. My partner Mal here quit his job and a secure life, and took three different loans from banks in his own name. We have jeopardized our lives, the trust of our friends, the trust of our families, just so that we could start this. There have been times when there was absolutely no hope that we'd actually be able to keep this company afloat.

'My mum is still forcing me to do an MBA and I still don't get more than four hours of sleep, because I just can't sleep. Everyone is talking about this great country of ours and how it's the world's fastest growing economy and let me tell you, I have tremendous faith in this great country of ours—

but that faith begins to shake when I meet people like you. People like you who tell me I can't do this. My aunty who constantly mocks me for taking this route. My mum who is actually depressed because I don't have a stupid tech job. My friends who think I'm stupid for putting all this money into something like Alma Mater at this age.

'Mr Ram, it is because of people like you that we don't have guys like Steve Jobs or Mark Zuckerberg here. It is because of people like you that every business idea that is new here has to be ripped off from the US. I feel ashamed and sad that I'm actually at the mercy of dimwits like you who think only someone above the age of thirty-five can run his own business. Mr Ram, you're forgetting, a man gets his balls at the age of thirteen and not thirty-five.'

The entire office went silent. Mr Ram had a lot of young interns working for him. They all stood up in disbelief. One of them started clapping and then everyone joined in. They must have clapped for like a good two minutes.

Wow. That felt good, but I suddenly felt someone screaming my name.

It was Mal. 'Dude, dude, where are you?' I was brought back to my senses. I was hallucinating, but how I wished I could have actually said all that to him!

'Guys, listen to me,' Mr Ram said, looking at both of us. 'There is not much of a future here. The rest is up to you.' And with that he left.

We were completely dejected. We had invested a lot of faith in this guy and we had paid him a lot of money. And this is what he predicted—₹75 lakh. Based on this valuation, even if we were to give 20 per cent of our company to an investor, we would get just ₹15 lakh, which would get used up in no time. I was broken. I had lost all my friends, my mum no longer believed in me and now this guy was telling me my company was not worth his time. I was at an all-time low and I was very close to slipping into a state of depression.

I didn't go to work for the next few days. We still hadn't moved into a new office, so I basically remained cooped up in my room. I slept for long hours. Mal, meanwhile, hadn't given up hope and continued to look for new financial experts. I just slept all day and all night. It was like a drug that would save me from all the strain I was going through then.

Get Busy Living or Get Busy Dying

After spending about a week like this, I got a message form an old acquaintance. His name was Rajiv Damodaran. He was a senior of mine from school. He had been the school captain and one of the most respected seniors ever. He said he wanted to meet me. I could not say no to him, so in spite of being in this zombie state of mind, I forced myself out of bed.

We met at a nearby Barista and got talking on a variety of topics.

'So Varun, how is the company doing now?' he enquired.

'Not too well, Rajiv. We are stuck because we need more money.'

'That's not a reason to worry. Every growing company needs that,' he said, sipping his cappuccino.

'Yeah, but we need a lot and our valuation hasn't come out great,' I said.

'What? Are you kidding?'

'No, Rajiv.'

'Varun, your valuation ought to be super high. You're in e-commerce man. That's the future,' he said.

'So we thought, dude. But apparently not,' I said.

'Varun, you're being naïve. Who did your valuation?'

'Mr Ram.'

'What? Why did you go to him? He has no clue about the internet business.'

'We heard he was one of the best in his field,' I shrugged.

'For old businesses maybe, but he won't understand e-commerce.'

'Are you serious?' I said.

'Yeah Varun, how much did he pitch you at?'

'₹75 lakh.'

To this day I can't forget the look Rajiv gave me.

'Ha ha, dude, you must be joking, right?' he said. 'Don't worry. I'll do something.'

I wore a defeated look.

'Don't be so dejected, man. This is life. Sometimes you're up and sometimes you're down. I suggest you read this book on Steve Jobs. Then you'll know what life truly is,' he said.

Rajiv was so right. How could I be getting dejected and hopeless in the face of a small adversity like this? Imagine what all Steve Jobs would have gone through.

Rajiv soon took it upon himself to get us the right valuation. He also said he would bring in a couple of financial experts who were 'very good' with these matters. Suddenly, I didn't feel like a zombie anymore. I felt better, if only marginally.

I went back home and opened the blinds. I started checking all the emails and finishing up the work that had piled up. We couldn't give up that easily, could we? I logged on to Facebook after a long time and was flooded with notifications. I started checking them one by one but one thing startled me.

You have 1 friend request.

It was Devika. How in God's name did that happen? I obviously clicked YES and, to my disbelief, she had given me full access to her profile again. This couldn't be true. God was definitely playing some game with me for sure. I mean, first Rajiv in the morning and now this. Could all of this really be true?

I was still online on Facebook chat when I was suddenly pinged by Devika. I had to slap myself again just to check if this was for real.

Devika: 'I never congratulated you for Alma Mater and the awesome, awesome website. Congratsss. ☺☺☺'

Three smileys? Wow.

Me: 'Thank you, Devika, I'm glad you liked it.'

Devika: 'Liked it?? Loved it ☺.'

Me: 'Oh thanks, Devika, that's very kind of you.'

Devika: 'He he, this is really awesome stuff.'

Me: 'Ha ha. Thanks so much.'

Devika: 'Okay, so mister, where's my hoodie?'

Woah. This is definitely going somewhere. Play it sensibly here.

Me: 'It's with me obviously.'

Devika: 'So when am I gonna get it?'

Me: 'Well, when you meet me.'

What??? Did I just type that??

Devika: 'Ah, I see. I could just order it, you know.'

Me: 'That could take four to five working days.'

Devika: 'I'm in no hurry, you know.'

Why do girls play so hard to get?

Me: 'Okay, so then order it.'

Devika: 'Aww, I didn't say that.'

Girls, Girls, Girls.

Me: 'Then?'

Devika: 'Do you have it in brown colour?'

Me: 'For sure.'

Devika: 'Yaaay!'

Me: 'So, when? Where?'

Devika: 'Hmmm…'

That was the longest Hmmm of my life.

Devika: 'Millers 46? Friday?'

Me: 'Done.'

Devika: 'Okay, gtg, so Friday then. Byeeeee.☺☺ X'.

Woah. She Facebook hugged me.

What surprised me was that there was not a single mention of Sid. Had she forgotten everything? I hoped she had.

The Greatest Day of My Life

While I was still on Facebook, I saw some pictures of Rohit, Gujju Boy and Sid at some party. As expected, I got senti and had to meet them at any cost. I called up the boys and told them not to fuck around and to meet me at Satya Bar and Restaurant. I didn't call Sid.

After two drinks, Rohit broke the silence.

'Dude, it's time you stop this silly fight man,' he said.

'I know da Varun, no point in going on like this,' Mehtu added his own two cent's worth.

'It's been six fucking months since you guys spoke to each other. Do you know how stupid is that?' said Rohit

'Dude, you remember in eighth standard, during the final exams, Sid took one of your answer sheets to copy from? And he got caught and the teacher kept asking who he got the sheet from. He never sneaked on you, dude. And remember how screwed he got, like he almost failed?' Mehtu added.

Rohit jumped in, 'And remember when during the twelfth standard boards, you needed the Chemistry notes and how you almost had a nervous breakdown because you weren't confident before the exam. Dude, it was Sid who photocopied those notes at one in the morning and gave them to you. And the exam was the next day. He didn't have to do that.'

After a long silence I finally spoke.

'Guys, that is true but he broke my trust—all the trust that I had in him. He went and told my darkest secrets to a complete stranger—and that too to the girl I really liked. Imagine that. Friendship is all about trust, right?'

'I know, bob,' Rohit intervened. 'But you can't hold a grudge against him for so long. Both of you have been friends for too long to throw it away like this.'

Whatever said and done, I really wanted to be friends again with Sid. I mean this guy had been my best friend since I was like ten.

'Hmmm', I finally said, after five minutes that seemed almost like an hour.

The boys knew that was the cue and Sid emerged from the vicinity. The bastard had been hiding two tables away all this while. Rohit got up as though he was a divorce lawyer who had successfully brought a couple back together. He took our hands and made us do a handshake in front of the entire crowd at Satya's. If that wasn't gay enough, the crowd started cheering. These bastards didn't even as much as clap when I had delivered my great monologue and now they were cheering when two boys were being brought back, as though they were lovers.

Sid and I sat down. We didn't speak much. There was so much to talk about, we didn't know where to start. But we soon started drinking and things were normal in a nanosecond. Rohit and Gujju Boy started singing *'jumma chumma de de'* which pretty much summed up the scenario from then onwards.

No matter where you are, no matter what you do, I guess life is absolutely nothing without friends. We all went to Sid's house after Satya's and crashed.

Thank God It's Friday

It was finally Friday—date day with Devika. The best day of the week. Haven't you always felt a tingle in your heart when it's Friday? I mean it is easily the best thing that happened to a week. Though its reputation has completely been ruined by this annoying little singer called Rebecca Black, it is still my favourite day of the week.

I still couldn't believe Devika had added me on Facebook and I still couldn't believe she had started a conversation with me. I mean, Bangalore women don't do that. Not like this was my first date or something, but I was obviously nervous. I just about managed to get the orders picked by Aramex by 7.30 p.m. and ran for a quick shower. I got dressed and was out of my house by eight o' clock. I took my mum's car, in case Devika needed a drop back home or something.

Millers 46 is a famous steak house in Bangalore. Bangaloreans love their sizzlers and not many places here do them as well as Millers. Their buffalo steak is to die for.

I had already reserved a table for two and was well on my way. Okay, actually I was like half an hour away and the crawling Bangalore traffic added to my misery. While I was still on my way, I got a text message from Devika.

'Hey, be there in 10 ☺'

Fuck. I had ten minutes to be at Millers and the traffic was definitely not helping. I mean if I show up late on our first date, it's going to get fucked, right?

I just about managed to get there by 8.35. I was already five minutes late. That was not too bad but I was still not inside the restaurant yet. I was frantically trying to find parking. Getting a parking slot in Bangalore is like finding a casino in the Himalayas. It was now 8.45 and I was a good fifteen minutes late, which was definitely not good for a first impression.

I finally managed to get into Millers by 8.50. I was wondering if she would even want to meet me after this delay. I entered the restaurant and scanned the crowd for her. Had she left? I kept looking but still couldn't find her. My stupid scanning took a full three minutes and by now it was 8.53.

And that's when I saw her. Tucked away in a cozy little two-seater in the corner. She looked way more beautiful in reality than in her pictures. Her long brown hair, her pretty eyes and that childlike innocence. Oh, I could just stand there and watch her but it was 8.55 and I couldn't even think of any excuses for my delay.

I finally reached the table. She looked up.

'Varun?' she said.

'Devika, Hi...'

'Hey!' Her smile was like a million bulbs had lit up. She looked alluring in a burgundy silk top and jeans.

I shook her hands. I was wondering if that was too physical too soon.

'I'm soo sorry,' I gushed.

'Hey, that's no problem at all,' she said.

'No, I got stuck in this jam, and then I couldn't find parking...' I rambled.

'Hey, don't worry about it. It's cool.'

My heart started beating faster.

'So...well...,' she said.

I got fucking tongue-tied. Awkward moment no.1.

Luckily, the waiter materialised and gave us the menu.

Waiters are always the central character in any date sequence.

'I love the sizzlers here', I said.

'I know, right? Me too,' she said.

'Have you tried the chicken wings?'

'I love them, yum.'

'Oh and the sizzling brownie!' I continued.

'I loove that.'

We seemed to agree on our choice of so far so good favourite dishes at Millers. We placed our order and got down to talking again.

'So, how's the new company going?' she asked.

'It's good, it's been crazy since we started but it's awesome.'

'I know, it is so cool, Varun,' she remarked shyly.

'Thanks, Devika.'

'You know, I've known about you for a long time.'

'Me? How?' My heart started racing again.

'You know Riya, right?' she said.

Riya was my friend from tuition. Sid dated her like a year back but broke up in three months. Her mentioning Riya made me slightly nervous.

'Yeah, I know Riya very well, what did she tell you?'

'Well, stuff…'

Why can't women just come to the point?

'Like…?' I persisted.

'General stuff, nothing important.' Devika shrugged her shapely shoulders.

Again, just when things were getting interesting, the waiter butted in with our order.

The food looked so divine that we stopped talking for a while. I mean I'm no glutton, but the spicy chicken wings… yumm. Woah! It was difficult to control.

'Oh I just love the chicken wings here,' she said. Even the way she ate them was so pretty.

'So tell me about this Riya thing,' I said

'Hmm…nothing much. So your friend Sid used to date her, right?'

Okay, this was getting really serious. Maybe she will talk about Sid now.

'Oh yeah, but that was very short-lived.'

'I know. I felt so bad. They looked so cute together.'

'Yeah, but I guess it wasn't meant to be,' I said philosophically.

We finished our main course and were now waiting for the sizzling brownie. This was going to be interesting because we had ordered just one. So we were going to share one and I was really looking forward to that.

All this while she kept playing with her hair, making my heart skip a billion beats. Oh, I could sit for hours just watching her.

'So you were telling me about what Riya told you,' I said.

'No, nothing…it's really silly.' Devika crinkled her nose cutely.

'But I want to know.'

'Aww, it's really nothing… okay, anyway, where is it?' she suddenly changed the topic.

'Where is what?' I said.

'My hoodie dude.'

Oh shit. Oh shit. In all this chaos I had forgotten the most important thing. Shit, Shit, Shit.

'Oh, yes, uh, the hoodie, uh.' I blinked stupidly.

Think of an excuse. Fast, fast.

'You forgot?' The expression she gave could break a million hearts.

'Uh, no uh…'

'Never mind, next time?' she said.

Boy! This was actually good. We had set up our next date because of my stupidity. This was good.

'But you're really sweet, you know,' she said.

'Me, why? I didn't even give you your hoodie.'

'No, just…' she blushed and looked away.

Aww, I could die of love right there.

And then again when things were getting a little mushy, the stupid waiter arrived with the cheque.

I obviously laid my rights upon the bill.

'No, you can't pay,' I said

'Why?' she asked with a hurt expression as if I had just insulted the whole of womankind.

'Because I requested for the meeting.'

'So?'

'Please…,' I said.

'No. We go Dutch,' she firmly said.

I just don't understand women at times. They always complain that men are not chivalrous these days and when we guys actually do something chivalrous, their feminism comes out to defend itself.

We finally left Millers at 11.30 and it was really nice and cold outside.

'Hey, how have you come?' I asked.

'Auto, I'll get one here, don't worry,' she said.

'There is no chance you're going in an auto.'

'What? No, I'm going by an auto. You think women can't go alone in an auto at night?'

She was definitely the feminist kind.

'They could but not at 11.30 at night. Please let me drop you,' I said.

She looked at me for like two minutes.

'Fine,' she finally said.

Phew. Yes, I was dropping her back home. Chivalry is not dead.

The drive with Devika was one of the best drives I have ever had in my life. There was hardly any talking. There was 'Tiny Dancer' playing on the radio, there was a light drizzle outside and both of us were soaking in the beautiful weather. Okay, fine. 'Tiny Dancer' was not playing on the radio but man, this was easily the best date I had ever been to.

Devika stayed in Frazer Town, which was very close to Millers and so our awesome little drive came to an abrupt end very soon. I finally stopped near her house.

She then looked at me again.

'Varun, I had a really nice time,' she said.

Nice time? I had the best time of my life here.

'Yeah, it was nice, Devika.'

She was about to leave and put an end to this blissful night. I didn't know how to stop her, I didn't want her to go, I wanted her to stay in my car forever.

And just then she stopped. She turned to me again.

'You remember I kept talking about Riya?' she asked.

'Yeah...'

'You know she dated Sid right?'

'Yeah,' I said, wondering where this was going.

'So Sid used to tell her how you had this huge crush on me,' she said.

Oh Fuck.

'Uh...no, nothing like that...,' I said, afraid to meet her gaze.

'He also told her everything you said about me,' Devika continued.

'Uh, well...'

'I thought that was really sweet.'

Silence. There must have been like two full minutes of complete silence. Save for the stupid dog barking in the background, the moment was simply magical. Just like the movies.

Then she leaned towards me.

And then, WE KISSED.

We must have kissed for like a good two minutes. And then without saying a word she started to leave.

As for me, my heart was signed, sealed and delivered. God, how am I going to sleep ever after this?

Before she left I asked her casually, 'Hey, but I thought Sid told you all this at Cirrus one night when he was drunk.'

'Oh yes, I vaguely remember him talking but I was pretty smashed myself so I don't remember much.'

'What? But you deleted me from Facebook after that, right?'

'What? No...why would I do that?'

'But I couldn't find you on my friends list nor could I search for you,' I said.

'Oh yeah...I disabled my account for this entrance exam I was studying for. But I got it back up a month ago. Okay, I gotta go now, I think dad has woken up. Bye.' Devika waved and ran to her house.

Oh fuck. What had happened between Sid and me was the stupidest thing I had ever done. There was so much I wanted to tell him but I just couldn't put the thoughts in words. I finally decided to send him a text with just three words: 'I am sorry.'

A Million Dollars? Are You Serious?

After a few days, I got a call from Rajiv at around eight in the morning asking me to meet him at once. Surprising as it may sound, even after we started the company, I had never seen this hour in the morning. I just about managed to get out of bed and rushed to the MG Road Barista where he was waiting.

I entered the place and saw Rajiv sitting at one of the tables. He saw me and broke into a broad grin.

'Varun,' he remarked casually. 'How's your morning?'

If only he knew.

'Good Rajiv, how's it going?'

'Very well, and it's going to get even better for you.'

'So you heard from the finance guys.'

'Yup.'

My heart started beating very fast.

'And…?'

'Not so soon, let's have some coffee first.'

'Uh, coffee, uh ok…'

After a long and excruciating wait, he finally spoke.

'Okay, so dude, here's the thing. Those valuation experts I was telling you about. Well, firstly they were super impressed with your company. They loved what you guys had done and they went through your numbers and everything. You both will have to come in for a detailed valuation though. But they gave me a figure based on what they saw.'

My heart started beating even faster.

'And that is?' I said.

'Well, it's a good number but I think you can get more.'

'But what's the number? I...'

'Because when I looked at everything I thought you could...,' Rajiv continued.

'Rajiv...,' I was getting impatient.

'And you know the potential for this is like crazy.'

'Rajiv...'

'And I truly believe... '

'Rajiv, dude...what's the number...?' I screamed, making heads turn in the coffee shop.

'Around ₹5 crore.'

My heart stopped.

'What?'

'Yes, pal.' Rajiv smiled.

'That's a million dollars, dude.'

'Yup.'

I couldn't believe what I had just heard. I called up Mal and asked him to come to Barista at once.

Mal was there in like five minutes flat. Rajiv repeated the entire spiel to him.

'Dude, are you fucking serious?' Mal asked him.

'Guys, you have a great thing going on here. Never go to people like Mr Ram. This is your right valuation, maybe even more.'

Mal and I were absolutely dumbstruck.

Okay, just to let you guys know, it was not like Mal and I were—or are—millionaires or something. Our company was only being valued at that figure. This meant we could give away 20 per cent and get around 80 lacs to help sustain our growth. So if you guys have this image of Mal and I driving our Porsche and living in a house like the ones on MTV Crib and all, then you will be very disappointed. But we hope to get there someday.

After meeting Rajiv, we went to celebrate at Shiva's with our customary chai and Milds. We were not millionaires, but we did have a million dollar company. And that felt bloody good to know.

Over the next few days, things improved drastically. We finally found an office space in Koramangala. It was a small little bungalow tucked away in a leafy little neighbourhood. We hated those tech parks with all those ID cards. We never wanted any of that.

The good thing about our new office was that it was like home. We finally had a place for ourselves and we spent some time getting nice furniture, getting the flooring done, creating a little sign board by framing a beautiful collage of all our pictures and mounting it on our wall. The dream was finally becoming a reality—we finally had our very own Alma Mater office and there were more goodies in store.

A few days later, we got a call from the Young Turks Show from CNBC.

Young Turks is one of CNBC's longest running shows; it puts the spotlight on young entrepreneurs poised to become tomorrow's leaders. The show traces their journey from who they were to who they have become. For the last eight years, this four-time award winning show has put the spotlight on the achievements of over eight hundred young dynamic men and women who have pushed the envelope to achieve the impossible.

Guests who have been featured range from first generation entrepreneurs in different fields like Vikram Akula of SKS Microfinance (named as one of Time Magazine's 100 most influential people), Aditya Mittal of ArcelorMittal, Rajiv Bajaj of Bajaj Auto, Rajiv Samant of Sula Wines, Malvinder Singh of Ranbaxy and a host of other first and second generation entrepreneurs.

'Mom, We're on TV'

A few days later when the show was going to be aired, my mum, being a true Indian mother, called up every possible friend and relative of hers and sent out umpteen messages to make sure no one missed her son on TV. I guess in India it really doesn't matter what you achieve, what you do, how much you earn, etc., so long as you come on TV.

Obviously, every channel has a brand value. An appearance on Star TV, Sony, Colors etc. will earn you high respect among the aunties and relatives. An appearance in reality shows has also got a very good standing these days. A Channel V or MTV will make you popular among your friends. In comparison, news channels obviously play second fiddle. So my appearance on CNBC had already isolated the masala-loving aunties— Anu Aunty in particular. Also, what the show was about was completely inconsequential to them. Basically, if you're not on *Indian Idol*, you don't count in the celebrity sweepstakes.

'Anu, did you see?' Mum asked excitedly, after I came on TV.

'Haan, we saw,' said Anu Aunty grudgingly. 'At first I couldn't find the channel only ya. Arjun had to tune the TV to set it.'

'Oho! It is easy to find ya.'

'I tho only watch Aaj Tak ya. It was a little boring in the middle and Varoon was wearing that dull sweater.'

'I know. I told him to wear something bright but you know boys these days ya.'

'And his friend has a beard no? And the programme was too short ya Poo. Sirf dus minutes, I think.'

'Nahin. I think it was at least fifteen minutes,' objected my mum.

'No Poo. It came and went. I hardly saw Varoon.'

'No, but he was there.'

'Arre, he's your son, even if he's not there you'll imagine it. Chalo, anyway, he came on TV. Next time tell him to come on Sony and then I will show my neighbour Rohini also. You know these NDTV people once took an interview of Arjun.' (It was for one of those programmes where these news crews find you on the road and ask for your comment.)

'Sachhi?' said my mum.

'Yeah. But you know I don't like publicizing ya. I don't have time to tell people only. Chalo, I'll rush, and tell Varoon this and all is okay but no MBA, no future.'

But my mum didn't care what Anu Aunty actually said. Her son was on TV and he had a million dollar company. Strangely, I never heard the word MBA from her again.

Back to Noon Wines

That night, all of us decided to meet at Noon Wines again. We were going there after almost a year. We had decided to meet at nine. I got a call from Sid when I was still on my way.

'Bastard, where you?' he barked.

'Dude, gimme five minutes,' I said.

'Dude, Devika is here.'

'Ha ha, what crap. She is with me.'

Sid turned to the rest of the boys. 'Okay, he's going to come in half an hour,' he said.

I finally reached the place in about twenty minutes. Everyone was in attendance. There was Rohit, who now had been accepted into the prestigious MBA programme at Tuck University; there was Gujju Boy who had not only made it to MIT but had also been awarded a 60 per cent scholarship which was quite unheard of. And there was obviously Sid, who had done something that had shocked us all. He had joined his dad's business in Chennai and was leaving the city soon.

Mal reached soon after me. All of us were under one roof, drinking together after a long time. We didn't speak about business or work or anything. We just did what we do best on such occasions. Get smashed.

Mal and I stepped out of Noon Wines for our customary smoke. We got our smokes and sat down. Both of us didn't utter a word to each other. We then saw a guy wearing one of our hoodies walking past us. Just a year ago we were at the same place talking about our grand idea and now we saw a complete stranger, our customer, actually 'wearing' our idea. It was a surreal moment.

We realised then that the real challenge had just about begun for Mal and me.

But one thing that really makes me happy and proud is that we actually went ahead and made a business out of the idea. Personally for me, this has been the greatest aspect of my entrepreneurial journey.

Like Steve Jobs famously said, '*We're here to put a dent in the universe. Otherwise why else even be here?*'

And with all due respect, Anu Aunty can go jump.

Looking Ahead...

Things have drastically changed—for the better—from the time of writing this book. Alma Mater has gone from being a two-man team in 2009 to fifteen employees and two offices today. We have worked with over 500—and still counting—schools and colleges. We have over 1,00,000 fans on our Facebook page, people who believe in our idea as much as we do. The best part is this is just the beginning and there's a whole lot left to do.

However, despite the success we have tasted, the entrepreneurial scene in India has yet to come of age. We still can't boast of eighteen-year-old inventors, or twenty-four-year-old billionaires. Sadly, there is no place for college dropouts like Bill Gates or Mark Zuckerberg in our country.

But the likes of Mal and me shall persist, no matter what the naysayers shall say. A day will come when India will become a teeming ground for entrepreneurs; when our students will be encouraged to learn and not mug; to lead and not follow;

to think and not blindly write exams. Entrepreneurs like me can't wait to see such a day. That is when we can truly say that the likes of Anu Aunty have been vanquished.

Postscript

Section A

'Will You Teach My Class?'

A few days after we came on TV, I got a call from a professor of a prominent business school. He wanted to know if I would be interested in delivering a guest lecture on entrepreneurship. Apparently, a friend of mine had suggested to him that I would be ideal for the job. I was quite amused, but also thrilled and flattered. What if I could convince this hotshot lot to quit their prestigious MBA programme? While such silly thoughts filled my head, my mom was wondering why I was getting my blazer dry-cleaned. Sadly, there was someone else present in the room—Anu Aunty, who thought it quite absurd that I should be speaking—that too before MBA student! She couldn't believe it.

'What will you tell them?' she demanded.

'I dunno, I haven't decided yet.'

'First you learn, Varun, then you teach.'

'But aunty, I think I can speak a little about...'

'Anyway, now you have to go. They have called you. These kids of today think they know everything, Poornima,' she was clearly rattled by my success.

I decided to forget about Anu Aunty and focused on preparing myself, gathering my thoughts on what I would say.

And thus, I went and suddenly found myself in a hall full of MBA students. It wasn't tough to guess they weren't happy to see me. I mean I was twenty-three but looked eighteen.

Guess what I spoke about? Anu Aunty, of course! I centered my talk around how she represented a strong force in this country that prevents youngsters from doing what they want. That really got the students' attention. I guess a lot of them have had 'Anu Aunty' moments, because they really seemed to connect with the whole thing. What's funny is a friend of mine recently faced an 'Anu Aunty' incident of her own. But that's another book.

I'm sure a lot of you must be facing this too. But don't let any Anu Aunty stop you from doing what you want to do. Dick Costolo, founder of Twitter, famously said—'The key is to just get on the bike, and the key to getting on the bike…is to stop thinking about "there are a bunch of reasons I might fall off" and just hop on and peddle the damned thing. You can pick up a map, a tire pump, and better footwear along the way.'

Section B

Ten Tips to Start Your Own E-Commerce Company

So, you have just quit your job and are at home contemplating your future. You tend to go to bed late and get up late. You spend most of your time looking at other people's profiles on Facebook. Well then, it's time to start an e-commerce company! I'm not going to tell you what everyone already says—get an accountant, manage your finances, think it out, ask people for advice, and so forth. I'm just going to share a few things I have learnt about running an e-commerce business.

1. If you have an idea, go ahead and do it. Don't tell your parents (they'll never agree), don't talk about it to your CEO Uncle (who will first ask you to create an in-depth business plan) or your friends (who will suggest sticking to a job). Get an accountant (use Justdial if you don't

know one), register the name (register your domain on Godaddy.com). All this without your daddy knowing about it—mine didn't know about Alma Mater until three months into business.

2. Get a business card of your company made that says CEO or whatever you want. Hand these out to everyone.

3. Remember the money you stashed away for travelling or to buy an expensive camera or what not? Put it into your new business. Trust me. At least you don't have to spend ₹40 lakh on an MBA.

4. Get a good designer to make your website. Remember, your website is your store. You have to make sure it's the best. Flip out your Berry and call all your friends who can design. Ask them to do it for half the price but make sure the quality is even better than what they would do for their full quote. Lure them with your passion. Tell them how this will be the Next Big Thing.

5. Sort out your operations. Make sure you have a good back-end system. Some common e-commerce platforms are Magento and E-commerce. Not only are these free but extremely functional and useful. Get your techie friends involved and ask them to build you a robust system. I'm telling you, techies love coding. They'll do it for free.

6. Promote yourself. If you want to start your company, you have to be shameless when it comes to marketing. Tell your friends to tell their friends, tag people you don't even know on your company pictures, go crazy on Facebook. I remember when we launched Alma Mater, people could only see Alma Mater pictures on their news feed for the

first week. We practically blacked out everything else. (Sorry for that, guys).

7. Talk to your customers. We still have our own personal numbers on the site. It could have been very easy for us to have a company phone number and fixed timings—say nine to five. But no, put down your own number. Talk to your customers, ask them what they think about the brand, ask them how they got to know about the company, ask them for suggestions to improve the service. The things you learn during these conversations are extremely important for your business.

8. Don't become bigger than the company. Just because you started the company (and automatically became the CEO), don't try to hire staff unless extremely necessary. In the initial days we used to personally go and man all our stalls. I've been a delivery boy, photographer, office boy, designer and played several other roles for the sake of our company.

9. If you have managed to read the above eight points then you will definitely start your own company. If you do, it is very important to follow point the next point.

10. Make me a partner.

Section C

Ten Things You Don't Know About an Entrepreneur

1. They orgasm every time they get an email on their blackberry. Well, almost.
2. You know that they call themselves CEOs. What you don't know is that they are also the gofers, office boys, drivers, interns and everything else for their companies.
3. They regard Microsoft Excel as the greatest invention of mankind.
4. They will ask for your business cards even before they get to know your name.
5. They will date you only if you live within a square mile of their office.
6. If you are a girl and have rich parents willing to invest in an entrepreneur's company, please ignore point no.5.
7. They will never complain about their boss.

8. Their parents never know what to say when someone asks them 'What does your son do?'

9. They will never pay you. Ever. They will, however, offer you a stake in their company even if that amounts to less than 1 per cent.

10. They will make you believe anything to sell something.